Voodoo Grasshopper

stories

"Blood Feast of the Astro-Wolves" originally appeared in *Schlock! Webzine* #7, Vol. 13 June 3, 2018. It was reprinted in *Schlock Quarterly, #5, Vol. 3. July 29, 2018.*

"Red Demon Versus the Worm People" originally appeared in *Schlock! Webzine* #30, Vol. 11 September 10, 2017. It was reprinted in *Schlock Quarterly, #3, Vol. 3. Dec. 23, 2017.*

"The Man at the End of the World" originally appeared in *Hellfire Crossroads 6*, First Edition, Midnight Street Press, 2017.

"Santa Claus and Bigfoot Versus Satan" appears here for the first time.

First Edition February/March 2020
Yellow Door Press

Cover Art/design: Neal Privett

Copyright 2019 Neal Privett

Printed in the United States of America

For my son…

Table of Contents

"Blood Feast of the Astro-Wolves!"

There is no place lonelier than a diner on a snowy night. Derek Beaumont thought this as he sat in the corner booth and studied the other patrons whose tired eyes betrayed the cold hard fact that they also had nobody waiting for them. He took another gulp of the thick hot coffee and paused from his beat copy of Aldous Huxley to stare outside the window at the falling snow. The night outside the little diner was silent and peaceful, a scene suitable for a postcard.

"Get yourself one more cup of java, ladies and gentlemen," the bus driver blared with a good solid smile that beamed from his cherry face like a light bulb. "We gotta get back on the road."

There were six other customers. An elderly man wearing a denim jacket and a ball cap from a stockyard. A couple of college kids with fur parkas. A well-groomed couple that looked to be in their mid-twenties. And a very pretty girl with sandy blonde hair, alone and maybe lost in the snowy night like Derek was. All passengers on the bus line destined for the west. Land of enchantment, Derek thought. Fresh start. From Chicago, through Minnesota and Wisconsin, and into the Great Plains. Then New Mexico eventually. With all the cheap diners and leg cramps you could stand along the way.

"So where you headed?" The voice startled Derek. The concept of speaking to the other passengers had never actually occurred to him. The elderly man in the denim jacket smiled at him from the adjoining booth.

"Out west. New Mexico."

"That right? What you gonna do out there?"

Derek thought for a moment. "I'm gonna write a novel." He winced at how cliché it sounded.

"Oh…a writer, eh? That's fine. What kind of stuff do you write?"

Derek groaned. "Well…I'm not exactly sure just yet."

The old man's response was interrupted by the sound of the burly cook clapping his hands to get everyone's attention. "Right this way, ladies and gents…you can pay your checks over here!" The old man forgot the burgeoning conversation with Derek and rose to leave.

The cook loomed over the counter with his meaty forearms that were a veritable museum of sailor tattoos. The grimy man was ecstatic with the scent of fresh money coming to him. Kind of like a shark smelling blood in the water, Derek laughed to himself. The people lined up, crowding the guy, as if they were afraid the bus would leave them. The register rang as the cook happily punched in the numbers and gave back change.

Derek closed his book. The girl smiled as she moved past him. Derek returned the smile, then turned back to the window. He remained in the booth, watching the snow fall peacefully outside. The passengers passed by, headed for the register. Derek didn't want to move. This was a nice place, an oasis in the night. The cups and saucers needed an oil change, but Derek loved little out of the way places like this.

The Lost America, where time didn't get the upper hand. He wouldn't be surprised if a zoot suiter or a leather jacketed greaser stumbled in. He glanced down at the table. It was a road map of ancient cracks, coffee stains, cigarette burns, and graffiti. It was *that* kind of diner, a time machine with ghosts, and he hated to leave. The bus was dark and cold, and all the hateful visions and lost dreams left behind would appear like specters out of the snowy night to haunt and scratch him. Sleep would come later, but only after a couple more hours of tossing and turning and trying to shut out the bitter cold with his frayed old jacket.

Derek sighed. Yes, there was no place lonelier than a diner on a snowy night with the knowledge that you had to leave and endure another cold sleep on a damned bus. And during those long cold wee hours, you had to take care not to drown in your own forlornness in the middle of the night ocean.

"Hey buddy…better move it! You are gonna get left behind," the driver bellowed. Another gulp of hot coffee waterfalled down Derek's throat and he slid out from the booth he had staked out for thirty good minutes and drifted towards the counter.

The blast of cold air made the passengers gasp as they exited the diner, leaving behind that island of warmth and light that had been their haven from the chilly bus, if only for an instant. The little bell on the door vibrated in the icy wind as everybody pushed past, shivering and pulling their coats and jackets tight around their bodies. They all rushed to get back on the bus, even though, if asked, everyone would have elected to stay. Derek followed the others as he always had, trailing behind everyone else with head full of unfulfilled plans and visions of books he would one day write but had never gotten around to. Maybe New Mexico would be the catalyst he needed to get started. Derek lifted his face up to the sky and smiled as the snow caressed his nose. God, he hoped so.

The light appeared from nowhere.

Like a blast of green atomic flash, *something*…big and traveling faster than anything they had ever witnessed before soared over in a lightning fast trajectory towards the waiting earth. The people stood there, frozen with disbelief. It was *a ship*…almost circular, with fin-like wings on the sides and flaring rockets protruding from the rear. A glowing ring of green lights encircled the front portal, through which Derek could have sworn he saw *occupants*…as incredible as it seemed…beings from another world piloting the descending ship through the snowy firmament!

The rockets from the craft were so hot that the falling snow melted instantly in the air and droplets of water rained down on the terrified people in front of the bus. Derek's thoughts exploded into a million mental shards and in an instant, all that pulsated through his mind was the animalistic frenzy of raw fear that jolted the bus passengers into panic after the initial shock wore off. Everyone raced back into the diner. The bus driver slammed the front door shut and screamed, *"We have to barricade this door!"*

The cook raced around the side of the counter, tossing his dishrag behind him. *"Jesus! Was that an airplane?"*

The driver pressed his body against the glass door and glared at the frightened cook. "That was no airplane, buddy! We're bein' invaded!"

"Jesus...hell!" The cook rushed over and fished a set of keys from his grease stained pants. He fumbled with them until he found the front door key. He moved the bus driver out of the way and locked the door. He shook it frantically to make sure it wouldn't open.

The diner was plunged into an awful silence...cold and motionless as ice forming on the eaves of a house on a winter's night. Everyone backed away from the front door and windows, their eyes glued on the strange green glow outside, emanating from behind the bushes beyond the parking lot.

The snow began to fall again. The passengers slowly found some of their lost nerve and one by one, as curiosity got the better of them, they stepped closer to the window to look. The row of bushes blocked any view of the fields beyond, where an unsettling glow flashed on and off through the haze of the snow.

Derek glanced at the cook. "What's back there?"

"Nothin.' Woods. A big pond."

One of the frightened college kids pressed his face against the window and groaned. "The U.F.O crashed back there!"

"What're we gonna do?"

The cook rushed to the counter and grabbed the telephone. "I'm callin' the police!"

The young husband growled impatiently. "About time someone did!"

The cook dialed the numbers frantically, then waited. He tried again and stood there with the color draining from his face. "Phone's dead!"

Everybody reached for their cell phones. Panic raged through the diner again when everyone realized that none of the phones worked. An unseen power had rendered technology useless. The cavalry was *not* coming. The people in the diner were alone and helpless…and they now knew it. Trapped in a roadside diner in the middle of the night with a spacecraft from another world sitting in the woods just over a wall of bushes.

"My phone's dead, too!"

"So's mine!"

"Does anybody's damned phone work?"

The jukebox went out next. Then the lights. A frightened hush took over the diner and everybody huddled together. "I got some candles," the cook said.

"Unlock the door…everybody get on the bus! We're leavin' *now*!" The driver motioned the cook over to unlock the door.

"*You're takin' me with you*," the cook cried out as he fumbled for his keys.

"Sure thing, Pops," the driver said. "Everybody load up!" The passengers started for the door, but the driver held out his arm and stopped them suddenly. "Waitaminute…I left the bus idlin'…it ain't runnin' anymore!" He pushed through the door and rushed over to the waiting bus, now a silent shell with frost already forming in the windows. After three attempts to start the engine, the driver gave up and returned to the safety of the diner. "I don't believe it," he said, with a defeated smirk on his face. "The bus won't start."

"You mean we're stranded here?" The young husband bellowed like a bull. "That's a great bus line you got!"

"Hey, buddy…that bus is tip-top! This makes no sense!"

"The phones don't work, either," the elderly man said. "Something isn't right!"

The stranded patrons pulled their coats and jackets close to their bodies and shivered. Everyone moved away from the front windows. The cook locked the door again and lit a half dozen candles. "Come on, everybody…have a seat and relax. Coffee's on the house."

The young husband sneered. "*Relax*? With aliens stalking around out there in the woods?"

"Someone will be along to help," the elderly man said. "The police...someone!"

"I sure hope so," the young wife said, emotion cracking her voice. Her husband pulled her close to him and kissed her forehead.

Derck glanced outside. "Rather than wait around, why don't we investigate?"

The others stared back at him in silence. The bus driver removed his cap and rubbed his head. "*Are you serious?*"

Derek shrugged. "What else can we do?"

The young husband snarled. "*You* gonna be the one to go, buddy?"

"Sure. I'll go."

The driver shook his head. "I must be crazy, but I'm with you."

"Me, too." Derek turned around to see the girl standing beside him, studying him with an admiring smile.

The young husband shook his head in disgust. "You're all crazy!"

The driver glanced back at the couple. "I don't see *you* doin' anything." He pulled the cap down over his face and zipped his jacket and nodded at Derek. "Let's go!"

A sudden gust of wind caught the door and almost ripped it from the driver's hand. The little bell sounded off again. The driver grabbed a flashlight from the bus, and they moved single file across the parking lot to the thick row of bushes. Derek couldn't speak for the girl or the driver, but a sick feeling bubbled up from deep inside him and for a moment he wondered if maybe the guy inside the diner wasn't right. Maybe they *were* crazy. But whatever his hesitations might have been, Derek pushed forward, pulling his scarf tighter around his throat and shielding his eyes from the blinding snow.

The three of them moved stealthily through the snow-covered parking lot, through the bushes and into the far woods. The terrain dropped down then rose steadily up again to a crest. The snow was deep at the very bottom of the gulley. The girl stepped down and quickly sank up to her waist. Derek watched her struggling for a second, then offered her a hand and pulled her free. She smiled in thanks. Derek found himself wondering what her name was. Maybe, if they all survived this, he would ask her.

No one spoke, but all three felt a shared and urgent sense of responsibility as well as a biting curiosity that was strong enough to propel them from the diner and into the night. Better to seek out the visitors and see what they wanted. At least that's what rolled through Derek Beaumont's mind as he pushed through the snow powdered pine branches towards the unknown. The stand of pines ended abruptly, and the hill rolled down again. Before them stretched the giant pond the cook mentioned earlier. The alien craft had skidded, then vanished beneath the water.

The pond was frozen solid except for a massive hole melted into the center. It was the point of entry for something very large and very hot. Steam rose from the pond and the surface quivered and bubbled from the heat of the ship's rockets.

"That ship crashed into the pond," the driver whispered. "Incredible! I wonder if the pilots are dead?"

Derek shrugged. "I don't know. Should we try to rescue them?"

"Look at the ice. The water in the center of that pond is scalding hot," the girl said. "I don't think it's possible until the ship cools. And by then it will probably be too late."

"I think we should go back to the diner," the driver said.

The girl was about to respond when she stopped and pointed at the ground on the far side of the pond. "*Look*!"

The driver pointed the flashlight in the direction of the ship. A trail of footprints in the snow led from the pond, up the bank and vanished into the trees on the far side. Beside it was another trail of prints. "Whatever is in that ship survived the crash and escaped into the trees."

Derek moved closer and examined the prints. "They look like some kind of animal."

The bus driver moved beside him. "Let me see. You know…this is really odd. These look like…*wolf prints*!"

The girl leaned in. *"Wolf prints*? Coming from the pond…from that ship?"

"I would know wolf prints anywhere. I grew up hunting in the Canadian woods. These are definitely wolf prints…I saw 'em a million times in the snow as a kid. These are big damned wolves…bigger than usual. And you know what else?" The driver scratched his chin and chose his words carefully before he spoke again. "Whatever made those prints was walking on *two legs!"*

Derek and the girl shot the driver an uneasy look. None of this made any sense. A real honest-to-God U.F.O had just crashed in the woods, piloted by *wolves* and they had walked away from the accident on *two legs* seemingly without a scratch.

The girl tried to break the tension. "Do you think maybe that the cook spiked the coffee with something?"

The driver broke out laughing, but only for a second. He shook his head and pulled his jacket closer around his body. "It feels like it just got 10 degrees colder. Let's head back."

"Let's see where those tracks go," the girl said.

The driver threw his hands up in surrender. "Oh, no…I'm done. You two go right ahead. This is it for me. I don't wanna find those things. My ticker can't take this much excitement." He lit a cigarette and walked back to the diner with a trail of grey smoke rising amidst the falling snow.

"I guess it's just you and me," the girl said.

"I guess so," Derek said. "We have to be crazy."

"No phones…no way to call for help. I think it's better to see what's out there. Maybe they mean us no harm."

"They…the two-legged wolf-people who rode in on that flying saucer?"

"Come on," the girl said. Derek followed her through the low hanging pine limbs that reached for the ground, held down by the falling snow. He shivered as a barrage of cold wetness slid down his collar. The night was freezing, but he knew that it wasn't so much the cold that made his teeth chatter, but the unseen possibilities of what lurked in the trees ahead.

Moonlight bathed the woods all around them, and Derek found himself lost in an otherworldly glow. Had it not been for the unnerving fact that alien beings had infiltrated their planet, the snowy woods would have seemed to him a peaceful scene from a long-lost childhood dream. But as it was, the freezing night hid unseen terrors that his quivering mind could only guess at. Wolf-like shapes, raced across the moonscapes of his imagination and when Derek wiped the blinding snow from his eyes, the trees in the distance loomed uncomfortably like waiting shadows. The wind picked up and the torrent of snow stinging their faces increased. The two bent their bodies to the cold and continued.

They picked up the trail of prints in the snow and followed. The pine stand rose to a rolling crest, then tumbled swiftly down an embankment. The girl took a step and slid to the bottom. Derek followed. He tumbled once and landed on his face below. The girl laughed, almost falling in the process. Derek blew the snow from his nostrils and mouth and picked himself up. He smiled. Let her laugh. It was a nice laugh. A clean laugh. And it broke the iron-coiled tension in the air around them.

The wolf prints stretched out before them, snaking through the low hanging pines. They brushed the snow from their clothes and kept moving.

The woods leveled off. In some places the knee-deep snow was packed tightly in against the trees like a blanket. Derek began to miss the coffee back at the diner. It tasted a little like old shoe leather, but it had been hot. He wondered if the girl missed the warmth and the bad coffee, too. He wondered other things…what her name was, where she was from, what she was doing riding a bus late at night, alone. The tracks in the snow continued. Where in the hell were these things going?

Derek stopped to rest. His breath rose into the air in steamy wisps. The girl glanced back. "Tired?"

"Just catchin' my breath. What are we gonna do if we find these things?"

"See where they go and what they want, I guess. Maybe they are here by accident."

"But what if they're not? What if they're invaders?"

The girl adjusted her toboggan and wrapped the scarf tighter around her chin. "Better to find out than sit around and wait on them to come after us."

The tracks led them deeper into the trees. They cut across a small stream. Derek's boots broke through the thin ice and water splashed on his jeans. He cursed silently as a shiver raced up his spine. The tracks continued through the pines to a large drainage pipe. Derek glanced up. "We're back to the road." He shined the light into the dark tunnel. The tracks continued through it and emerged on the far side in the snow.

Derek and the girl stopped dead in their tracks when they heard the howls. Two animalistic voices from another world, melding together into a terrible crescendo and rising high into the winter night. The girl reached for Derek and he pulled her close. They stood there in the drainage pipe with a savage chill running up and down their bodies as they held one another. The snow swirled around the end of the tunnel, the flakes dancing in the flashlight beam.

After a small eternity, Derek took the girl by her gloved hand and they moved through the pipe. A sudden lightning strike of fear exploded in Derek's brain when two large shadows rushed past. He threw himself back against the wall of the drainpipe and pulled the girl with him. They melted into the shadows and waited.

The things were out there!

Derek caught quick glimpses of them as they raced past. *On two legs!* The sound of heavy footfalls in the snow and the hard breathing of running animals filled the tunnel. Another savage howl rocked the night and the girl bit her fist to keep from crying out. Derek tried to control his panicked breathing, but the very sound of his own heartbeat louder than a drum and he wondered if the beasts could hear it.

After scavenging the low wet area beyond the pipe, the alien creatures vanished into the trees. Derek and the girl peered out cautiously and made sure they were alone before emerging. The snow was violently disturbed all around them. The beasts had been frantically trailing something. *"Let's get out of here,"* Derek whispered.

The sight of a freshly killed deer caught the pair off guard. The dead animal lay in a pool of its own blood straight ahead. The snow around the carcass was stained with crimson splashes. The creatures had killed swiftly and silently. And they had quickly devoured about half of the meat. Steam rose into the air, shimmering in the light of Derek's torch, and hot blood bubbled from deep within the stomach cavity, freshly ripped. A few snapped ribs protruded from the grisly kill.

Derek pulled the girl away and together they ran. They hurried across the low wet area, up the embankment, and onto the road. It was snowing even harder now. Everything was vanishing beneath a soft sheet of white. Derek and the girl started walking, leaning into one another for warmth. They halted a few steps later. The tracks appeared again in the flashlight beam, not yet covered by the fresh flakes. The things came from the woods and took the highway west. From the direction of the tracks, it appeared the beasts were keeping to the road. Derek looked around, trying to gain his bearings.

The diner was in that direction.

A chilling thought suddenly occurred to him. "What if they headed towards the diner?"

The girl clenched her teeth. "*God*, where is the sheriff when you need him?"

"We are so isolated here that I doubt anybody even knows the ship crashed but us."

The headlights of a car appeared ahead. The car rounded a curve and continued towards Derek and the girl. They signaled the driver to stop. But something was wrong. The car swerved out of control, coming right at them. Derek was about to grab the girl and bail off the embankment when the car swerved again and came to a crashing halt against a tall pine. Tons of snow barreled down upon impact, covering the windshield and roof of the car, a gold colored Dodge. Derek and the girl ran over.

The Dodge was still running. It was wedged against the tree, so it could not move any farther. The hood was completely caved in. The windshield was shattered in one spot. The sound of tinkling glass blowing in the wind and falling on snow filled their ears like a dirge. The front tires were flattened from the wreck. But the thing that caught Derek's eye was the gashes on the side of the door. Huge rips in the metal, as if made with claws.

"The windshield," the girl said. She gestured to the smashed back window. "The tree didn't shatter it." Something had reached inside the driver's window and smashed the man's head against the windshield. Derek peered inside the car and immediately wheeled around in horror. He retched for a second, then vomited in the snow.

The girl looked, too, and turned away. The man inside the car was dead. His head reclined at a weird angle on the seat's headrest. His neck had been broken, but not from the impact of the wreck. Three bloody lacerations rolled beneath the dead man's chin, laying open his throat. The man had not been dead long. Wet blood still bubbled from the gaping wound. The dead man's face was crushed in. His nose was completely gone. Spattered blood and bits of ragged flesh hung from the broken windshield glass.

Derek shined the light down the length of the corpse. His intestines lay in a pile beside him in the seat. The flesh around the man's chest and right arm showed the tell-tale signs of teeth. They had gutted him inside the car and had taken as many bites as they could before the car got away from them. The man was already dead before the wreck. The wolves must have hit him out of nowhere like an atomic bomb, breaking his body and ripping into his flesh with their razor-sharp claws.

The man sat in a twisted, awkward position. His right leg was broken and wedged up under the dash, keeping his foot stuck firmly on the gas pedal. That's why the car was still running. Derek reached inside the car and switched off the ignition. He opened the glove compartment and shined his light inside. It was there, as he had hoped. A gun.

Derek checked to see if it was loaded. *"Thank God,"* he said. "The poor guy never had a chance to use this. They must have hit him hard and fast."

Another howl echoed from deep in the night ahead of them. It was the sound of hunters, excited and lusting after blood. *Earth blood.* And it seemed human or animal did not matter.

"What if these things came here to hunt?" Derek mused. A terrible shiver twisted his spine, almost snapping his back as the words left him. "What if they came here from outer space for *meat*?"

"You mean *'open season'* on us?"

"Yes!"

"That's too terrifying to think about!"

They moved stealthily down the snow-blanketed highway towards the diner.

Derek held the girl tight and the gun tighter.

A hot rush of relief came over them when they saw the neon lights of the diner in the hazy distance. But their elation faded quickly when they saw the front door. The glass had been shattered. Pieces of plywood now covered the holes. Part of the large front window was missing as well. Derek could see a light dusting of snow that had blown in on the window side tables.

Derek called out. There was no answer at first. But after a moment, the familiar voice of the bus driver greeted their ears, partially muffled by the falling snow. "Is that you guys? God, I am glad to see you!"

Derek stepped over the broken glass and splintered wood. His boots crunched as he moved. "Is everybody okay?"

The bus driver frowned and gestured to two bodies covered with blood stained tablecloths.

The cook stepped out from behind the counter. Spatters of blood covered his wife beater. "*Goddamned monsters*! They hit the front window, bounced off…then they busted through the front door! We couldn't stop 'em!"

The elderly man walked over to Derek. He sighed with relief when he saw the old coot. The man shook his head frantically, as if he did not believe his own words, "*Werewolves*…that's the only way I can describe 'em! Werewolves in space suits!"

Derek glanced around the room, then back at the sheeted bodies. "*Who*…?"

The girl moved close to Derek and took him by the arm.

"The young couple," the bus driver said with a groan. Derek noticed the blood trickling through the cuff of the driver's leather jacket. Tiny droplets splattered on the tile floor. "One of the damned things bit me when I tried to brace the door. Came through on top of me."

"You alright?"

"I'm fine. Wrapped my arm up with a rag. That kid was a real jackass, but I didn't wish nothin' like this on him. Things ripped him and his little wifey to shreds with us beatin' 'em with brooms. The cook even hurled a meat cleaver at 'em. Didn't do no good."

Pools of blood ran together in the center of the floor. Small bits of raw meat were scattered amidst the broken glass. Derek spied something shiny and reached to pick it up. He recoiled in disgust when he realized that it was a human tooth.

The elderly man in the denim jacket pushed the cap back on his head and sighed. "Damn shame, those two kids!"

The wide-eyed college students in the parkas sat together at the bar, staring off into space. They were eaten up with fear; it had swallowed them whole and trapped them in its awful belly. They reeked with it and from the looks etched onto their traumatized faces, they would never escape this terrible moment, no matter how many years passed them by.

Derek lit up. "Hey…*that car*!"

The girl moved closer. "What do you mean?"

"The car that crashed into the tree…I can't believe I didn't think about it earlier! The car was *running*! It came from the direction of…what's the next town over?"

"Bakersville," the cook replied.

"The girl smiled. "So there's a chance that the saucer isn't controlling all of the machines and power in Bakersville…which means we can get help!"

"That's right," Derek said. "I'll go…bring back help!"

The driver frowned. He rubbed his wounded arm and shivered. "Kid…don't you think you've risked enough already tonight? You two were lucky the first time."

"Somebody's gotta go for help," the girl said. "Count me in, too!"

The driver coughed as another savage chill ran up his spine. "God…I think I'm runnin' a fever. It's that damned wolf bite."

The girl frowned as she lifted his sleeve to examine the wound. "It's infected. We'll try to find some antibiotics in Bakersville."

"Okay. Find the sheriff, too. Be careful," the driver said.

Derek handed the pistol to the driver. "Here…you might need this."

"You need it more," the driver protested. Derek nodded his head and moved towards the door.

"You kids watch out for those damned *monsters*," the cook added. "Straight there…straight back!"

"Tell somebody what's happening here," the old man said.

"I will." Derek said as the door swung open and they vanished into the snowy night once more. They moved steadily down the frozen highway, over the ridge, and down into Bakersville. Every dense patch of trees screamed at them and every shadow jumped out with fangs bared. But they made it into town a couple hours later without incident. Derek was relieved to see the town limits sign, but the thought of what might have happened if the wolves had found them along the way made his spine almost snap with a savage icy shudder.

Derek and the girl walked into town only to find it deserted. The snow beat against dimly lit buildings that betrayed no signs of life inside them. The kids moved, with the grinding sound of their boots in the snow, under the main traffic light in town, past the old post office, past the saloon and across Main Street before they stopped.

A howl resonated suddenly from the deep woods that surrounded Bakersville.

The terrified kids pulled close to one another and listened, with the breath frozen in their throats. Another triumphant howl rang out, echoing across the otherwise silent town. Derek felt his heart quiver and miss a beat inside his chest. Somewhere out there was a meat-eating horror from beyond the stars. A space-wolf with a predatorial instinct like its terrestrial brothers and sisters, but with the intelligence to build a ship and fly it halfway across the galaxy. Derek let the thought sink in until he couldn't bear it any longer.

"Come on," Derek whispered. They moved across the deserted street to the drug store.

The bell rang as they entered. The warmth welcomed them in and wrapped itself around their frozen bodies. Jazzy elevator music played softly over the speakers. Derek glanced around frantically. There was no one there.

The girl split off and moved cautiously up one aisle, then another. Derek found something for wounds and shoved capsules and bandages into his coat pocket. Then he moved past the toothpaste and mouthwash, past the magazine stand where Alfred E. Newman grinned mischievously back at him from the cover of *Mad Magazine*. He moved around the corner of the next aisle and almost screamed when he bumped into the girl. She blew a sigh of relief and gestured towards the counter. They inched their way closer and slowly peered over.

The girl gasped and turned away. A wave of nausea overcame Derek once more and he stumbled, catching himself on the counter before he collapsed. "*God*!"

Two corpses lay in a heap behind the counter, their throats torn out. One of them, Derek figured it was the pharmacist, judging from his blood-spattered white coat. The dead man was missing his eyes. The door behind the counter…which probably led outside, had been wrenched off its hinges and tossed aside like a section of cardboard.

The urge to flee hit them and they raced back outside. The grocery store was across the street. The automatic doors swung open and they rushed inside. Derek's heart sank when he realized that there was no one there, either. The two kids raced up and down the deserted aisles. It was as if everyone had just walked away.

The girl grabbed Derek's arm and motioned for him to stop when they moved past the meat counter. Bloody paw prints decorated the floor and inside the glass counters were splashes of red blood from the ripped open packages of raw meat. The wolves had been through there, devouring all the beef, chicken, and pork. Nothing was left.

The girl hesitated, then peered over the counter. No bodies were there. She motioned towards the swinging door beside the meats, where the freezers and stock were. Derek had the same thought: maybe there were survivors hiding back there.

The girl pushed through the swinging door, with Derek right behind her. The back room was quiet except for their snow-caked footsteps on the concrete floor. A single light bulb hung from the ceiling on a wire. Each wall was lined with cans and boxes draped in broken shadows. On the right was the freezer. A thin streak of light emanated from the cracked door.

Derek reached for the handle. A sliver of frost had formed on the door frame. He pulled it free and peered inside the freezer. The gore-soaked vision of about two dozen bodies assaulted his senses. Several corpses hung by meat hooks from the ceiling. Several were stashed on shelves, their dead eyes glazed over with frost and frozen wide with fear. A couple of people were cut into portions, their meat wrapped like steaks with paper. The girl glanced over Derek's shoulder before he could stop her. She wheeled around and fled the freezer. Derek slammed the door shut and ran after her.

He caught her on the milk aisle. She struggled against him for a moment; her eyes filled with panic. "*Calm down…it's gonna be alright,*" he pleaded until the girl finally relaxed and buried her face in his coat. Her sobs melded with his sobs and they stood there in the grocery story, shielding one another against the sheer horror they found themselves mired in.

"That was *deliberate*," she said. "Those things know what they're doing…they are here to hunt us and take our meat!"

"Too bad they're not vegetarians, right?"

She laughed and threw her arms around Derek's neck. Her lips met his and Derek knew that he was not alone in the night. Someone stood with him.

The snow had ceased falling outside. And the bone-chilling rays of a full moon ripped through the clouds, illuminating the deserted streets of a doomed town. The moon was so bright that the kids shielded their eyes from the silver glare as they turned the corner onto Market. The girl saw it first. Down the street was a police car…parked at the gas station.

They raced down the snow packed sidewalk and stopped short of the car. The wind blew a cloud of snow their way. Powdery sheets of white rained down from the roof of the station. The lights were on inside, but there wasn't a human to be found. Derek moved closer to the patrol car parked beside the pumps. A ticking bell sound greeted his ears and when he got close enough, he realized that the snow was melted around the tires. The nozzle lay in a heap on the pavement, spewing gallons of gasoline onto the ground. It pooled around the car and rolled in a steaming river towards the station, melting a swath of snow in its wake.

The officer lay slumped over the steering wheel. His head was missing and in its place was a bloody stump that oozed freezing gore. Derek reached into the car and took the officer's revolver. He checked to make sure it was loaded and shoved it down the front of his pants.

"There's nobody to help us here," he said. "We need to go!"

A loud crash made the kids take cover behind a gas pump. Derek's stomach twisted, and his heart turned to pure ice when he saw the outlines of two figures rummaging through the empty gas station. The sound of breaking glass filled the winter air and a severed head came rolling across the snow, coming to rest in front of the fuel pump the kids cowered behind. The glazed eyes stared blankly at Derek and blood pooled slowly around the nose and mouth, dribbling into the snow. Derek covered his eyes and tried to ignore the sickening horror before him. Another crash came from the station. The kids glanced up to see the wolf men piling bodies up before the door. One of the beasts pushed through the door with a limp body strewn across its massive shoulder.

It dropped the dead man atop two others and returned into the station.

Derek reached into his pocket and found a book of matches that he had picked up from the diner. He looked at the girl and winked, then rushed past the pumps, amid his companion's frantic whispered protests. He thought for a moment, glancing around. Three metal newspaper boxes sat on the sidewalk beside the door. All local papers. He jammed one of the boxes tightly under the door handle. A steady flow of gasoline covered the front of the station, enough to cause a massive explosion. He peered inside. The monsters were so busy investigating the interior of the station that they did not notice him. Wet, gasoline-soaked pawprints dotted the inside floor. He took a newspaper from one of the boxes and folded it, then he motioned for the girl to run.

Derek raced to a safe spot, lit the newspaper with the matches, and tossed the flame into the growing pool of gasoline. Great orange and blue fingers of fire appeared and swam the trail of fuel, right up to the front door of the station. The kids ran away as fast as they could. A massive explosion rocked the night a second later and knocked them sprawling face down into the snow. Derek looked back to see an Olympian tower of smoke and flame rise into the sky. The station was gone…in its place was an inferno, and somewhere in the midst of that destruction were the two lupine aliens. Derek silently prayed that they were incinerated, but somehow, he knew that it wasn't true. A sudden howl of rage and pain came from the burning ruins of the station and a tall figure engulfed in orange flame bolted from the fire and raced screeching down the road a hundred yards before collapsing into the snow. Derek paused for a moment, then walked over to the burning wolf man. He stood defiantly over the creature, watching its fur melt into nothingness and the flesh underneath bubble and sizzle.

The girl took his arm and stood beside him watching the monster cook. "Where's the other one?"

Derek glanced back at the station. "It's dead."

They waited a moment, to make sure that nothing else emerged from the wreckage, then they walked around the corner and found a blue pick-up truck on the street with the keys still in it. The girl climbed into the passenger seat and stared thoughtfully at Derek as he turned the key and the engine sprang to life. "Why is the power still on here?"

"Maybe the saucer took the power out back at the diner. Bakersville is a few miles away from the crash site. Maybe the energy from the ship didn't reach this far. Who knows?"

Something crashed into the side of the truck all of a sudden. The girl screamed and fell into Derek's lap. He shoved the gun towards the passenger window and gasped in amazement at the frightened and very human face staring back at him through the frosty glass.

The man beat frantically on the window and cried out, *"For God's sake…help me!"*

Derek reached over and unlocked the door. The man winced as he climbed inside. Derek noticed the bloody towel wrapped around his arm. "You're hurt," he said.

"One of them bit me." The man coughed violently. He shivered and gritted his teeth as a wave of fever wracked his body. Derek turned the heat up. The truck pulled away from the curb and headed out of town. Derek blew a sigh of relief.

The man continued, "They came outta nowhere…took over the town. Killed almost everybody. Started dressing them out…like *deer!*" The man massaged his wounded arm and stared out into the night. "Thank you for picking me up. I'm probably the last living person left in this town."

"We witnessed the handiwork of those things," the girl said.

"Where did they come from?"

"Outer space," Derek said.

The man shook his head in disbelief. "*Werewolves? From space?*"

"Looks that way."

"They're dead now. We blew them up at the gas station."

The man leaned back in the seat and grinned. "Way to go."

"Where to now?"

"Little diner the next town over. We got people waiting for us," Derek said. "We've got something for that arm, too."

The man lurched forward suddenly and cried out in pain. Derek pulled over to the side of the road. "Are you okay?"

"Yeah," he replied, in a half whisper. "Yeah…keep drivin.' I'm fine."

Something hit the truck suddenly and spun it around in the road. Derek regained control of the sliding Ford and pushed the gas pedal to the floor. The pickup sailed off into the darkness.

Something raced alongside, gaining speed. Derek recognized the tall, dark figure right away.

It was the other wolf! Rivulets of smoke rose from its charred hide and trailed off into the cold air. The creature was covered with burns, but it came after them with every ounce of rage and strength it had. The man screamed from the passenger side as the wolf-thing slammed into the truck, sending it skidding off into the ditch. Somehow Derek pulled the wheel and handled the truck back out onto the road. They kept moving. The beast came right at them again. This time Derek swerved and knocked the monster sprawling. It fell in the road, rolled, and came back at them.

The wolf slammed into the truck again. The girl glanced over at its horrible face, covered with hairless blistered flesh, pressed against the window. The hunter from other worlds…the child of other moons… howled defiantly and fell back. But it possessed otherworldly strength and agility and sprang over the back of the truck as if the vehicle were standing still. It vaulted over the hood and planted its feet firmly into the road, bringing the truck to a screeching halt as if it had crashed into a tree.

Derek pushed the accelerator, but the tires spun helplessly. The beast lifted the truck and howled, sputtering blood and foam across the hood. The monster growled and barked, gnashing its teeth at the humans helplessly trapped in the cab.

Hate-filled burning yellow eyes glowed back at Derek from a disfigured face. Pools of bubbling saliva formed around yellowed fangs in anticipation of the kill. Derek knew that they would not die easy.

"Cover your faces!" He screamed and aimed the gun at the beast's eyes…those terrible burning eyes! He pulled the trigger and a storm of breaking glass showered them. The wolf dropped the truck and fell back into the snow.

The truck bounced as it rolled over the top of the wolf-thing. Derek felt the bones crunch and the breath gurgle as it was forced from the thing's body. He stopped, threw the truck in reverse and rolled over it again. He pulled away and ran over the monster again and again until it was a pile of festering, steaming gore.

About a mile out of Bakersville, the wounded man lost consciousness. The girl tried to rouse him, but to no avail. Derek pushed the truck forward into the night…hoping that somehow the man's life could be saved back at the diner.

They pulled up at the diner sometime later, after many miles of darkness fed by fear, with the cold rays of the winter moon beating down on the truck. Derek threw the truck into park and hopped out, racing to the passenger side. He froze. The man had regained consciousness and glared at him through the frosted window. Derek shivered as he gazed into the inhuman depths of burning yellow eyes!

Patches of fur sprouted from the man's face and hands. Fangs jutted from his blackening lips and claws appeared on his upraised hands…the curse of the astro-wolves' infectious bite! Derek screamed at the girl, "*Get out of there*!" She sprang from the driver's side of the truck and scurried across the snow. Derek stepped back and aimed his pistol right at the man's face. He pulled the trigger and the wolf vanished amidst an exploding sea of glass and blood. The wolf man slumped forward and did not move again.

The power was still out in the diner. Derek and the girl stepped inside. The haunting glow of candlelight greeted them at the door. The girl slid her arm around Derek's waist. "Where is everybody?"

"I don't know…maybe in the back?"

"Kate."

"What?"

"My name is Kate."

Derek smiled and leaned down to kiss her. Now he knew her name…that soft, beautiful name that meant he wasn't all alone in that cold night on planet Earth. "Nice to meet you," he beamed.

Something came out of the shadows just before their lips met…something covered in dark fur that ripped the girl out of his arms and sent her decapitated head sailing over the counter and her body flailing in the opposite direction. Something that tore the life and the warmth from Kate… destroyed every moment that Derek could have shared with her for the rest of their lives. Something terrible that sent the woman he could have loved reeling into the next world without warning. Derek screamed when he recognized the bus driver's jacket. He emptied his gun into the wolf man's eyes.

Silence crept back into the diner.

When his eyes adjusted to the half-light, Derek noticed the splattered blood on the far wall. In the corner lay the dismembered fragments of the remaining passengers. All of them sliced into pieces by the monster's claws. Derek recognized the blood-soaked parkas of the college kids, the cook's tattoos, and the old man's denim jacket. His stomach felt as if it dropped a mile deep suddenly.

He dropped the empty gun and walked outside. He stood there in shock, staring up into the firmament. It was snowing again. Saucer-like ships with swirling green lights flew over. The sky was filled with them.

"Red Demon Versus the Worm People"

Red Demon carefully navigated the treacherous mountain roads in his Jaguar convertible, the thrill of another victory in the ring still resonating in his head. He groaned and massaged the soreness in his arm with his left hand, keeping the right on the steering wheel. Señor Guapo, with his bleached blonde locks and gleaming silver tights, had been a formidable opponent. The Americano was a pretty boy, but not to be underestimated. In one round, Senor Guapo had camel clutched, pile-drived, and head-butted Demon nearly senseless and he now felt the painful after-effects of the match as he drove the long and winding mountain road home.

But despite the younger rival's strength and agility, Demon had managed to pin him to the mat and now returned home a winner.

The luchador pushed the red sports car over the mountains as the moon painted everything in a silver glow and the night winds blew dreamily through the open top. With his crimson red mask and flowing satin cape, Red Demon would have been quite a sight for any passing motorists. The public loved him. His career was pushing twenty successful years. The ring…comic books…movies. The Demon was flying high in his native country. The fans were the best. Hearing his name chanted in the packed audience was a sacred feeling. He never grew tired of it.

The call came through just as Demon began the descent into the valley where his bungalow waited. He groaned. He wanted rest more than anything right now, but obviously this call was an emergency. Pushing thoughts of a hot bath and a good night's sleep out of his head, Demon snatched up the phone.

It was Professor Huerta. "Red Demon?"

"Yes, Professor?"

"Something terrible has happened! They have my daughter!"

A cold chill crawled over Demon's body like spiders in a tomb. "I am on it, Professor! Please don't worry!"

"I know that you must be exhausted after your match…but I need you! *Find Ana!*"

"I will, sir…don't worry…"

"They want *the book*, Demon!"

"Professor…I advised you to destroy that damnable book! Nothing but evil can come from its bloody pages!"

"I know now that you were correct, Demon! I have the text in my study. They left a note…demanding the book to be left at the mouth of the San Carlos cave at midnight tonight!"

"They cannot get that book in their possession, Professor…or the entire human race will be threatened!"

"That is why I am calling you, Demon! Get my daughter back from those fiends and I will destroy the book for good!"

"Don't worry, Professor! I will save Ana!"

"Thank you, Demon! Report back to me when she is safe!"

"I will, sir! Red Demon out!" The luchador placed the phone under the seat. All thoughts of sleep were forgotten. Now there was only the searing need to do his duty. He leaned forward and stepped on the accelerator. Up ahead was the unpaved road that led to the cave, a taboo place for the locals. No one ventured that far out and certainly no one dared to explore the dark recesses of San Carlos cave. He swerved to make the next left and took a sandy side road.

The famed luchador slammed on the brakes when the forbidding cave appeared ahead. The jaguar skidded, slinging sand in all directions. The car came to a stop a few feet away from the entrance. The cave loomed at the base of the mountain like a monster's gaping mouth, ready to swallow the Red Demon alive and grind his bones into powder.

Demon drew an anxious breath and trudged forward, though his uncooperative legs felt like jelly. Somewhere, deep in the darkness was the scientist's abducted daughter. And somewhere, lost in the forbidden regions of the earth's dark interior waited something else…

****

The book was known around the world as *The Necronomicon*…an ancient text that caused madness in those who possessed it. The book was taboo and had been used secretively for centuries for the express purpose of summoning demons and otherworldly deities. *They* wanted this book…the things in the cave. The mysterious creatures wanted the forbidden tome bad enough to kidnap the daughter of Mexico's most prominent scientist, the esteemed Professor Huerta, who had dedicated decades to the study of one text: The fabled Necronomicon. Written as a guide to summoning other diabolical worlds, The Necronomicon was written in blood by the mad Arab scholar, Abdul al Hazred in the 700s. The text was thought lost for centuries, until it turned up in Europe and then in the United States, finally arriving below the border much to the chagrin of Red Demon. The book was *trouble*…and he had warned the professor on more than one occasion to destroy it once and for all. There were some things that man was not meant to know.

And now beings from the world far beneath the earth plotted to take the Necronomicon. With it, they would summon The Old Ones; ancient, monstrous gods that had ruled the earth long before man was a twinkle in the eye of the cosmos and had retreated back to the cold stars from whence they came. Not only would the perpetrators from the cave summon these interstellar horrors back to earth, they would also open up dimensions closed for millennia, raise the evil dead, and unleash destruction on a scale unknown to mankind.

Red Demon could not allow that to happen.

****

The flashlight's beam cut through the darkness of the cave. The shadows were thick. They almost choked the breath from Demon's throat. But he continued onward, deeper and deeper into the earth.

His heart trembled when he realized that the air was growing colder by degree the deeper he went into the cave. He thought of the stars and the soft night above that had been so peaceful just a little while earlier. Now the upper world fell farther behind with every careful step he took.

The cave was a straight shot, at least for now. He wondered how he would ever find his way back out once the tunnels split off into different directions, vanishing into the mountain. Men had been lost forever following the disorienting curves of caves, their bones disappearing into darkness to become powder in some lost chamber far from the world of humans. Demon sighed and strengthened his resolve. He would not become lost. He would not fail. The doctor was depending on him. The fate of mankind itself depended on him.

Time seemed to stand still as the tunnel snaked through the ancient mountain. Demon shivered as icy drops of water fell from the ceiling, pelting him. Soon the narrow confines of the tunnel opened up into a great chamber and Demon could not help but pause and stare in awe at the stalactites and stalagmites reaching up from the cave floor and down from the sparkling ceiling. For the first time, the cave seemed to be another world, not just a forbidding hole tucked away from the eyes of man.

But despite the surreal beauty of this chamber, there still existed a gnawing sense of dread that permeated all. The cool stream that flowed over the smooth stone floor almost glowed a blood red in the light of Demon's flashlight. The glistening moisture of the walls seemed to him at that moment the gleaming eyes of a thousand devils lurking and the rock formations appeared to be their fangs, waiting to tear his flesh to shreds and rend his bones into powder. The luchador, moving with a hard-won caution nurtured by years of worthy opponents…in and out of the ring, pulled his glittered cape close around his bare chest and continued down through the cavern. Somewhere down there…beyond this enchanted chamber…the girl waited. Along with horrors unimaginable.

Demon wondered if the girl was still alive. Of course, she was. She had to be. Those things only had one bargaining chip and that was Ana. They wanted The Necronomicon and she was their only hope of obtaining it.

On the far side, the cavern began to shrink and finally descended into a cramped tunnel that turned downward into blackness. The strange beauty of the cavern was gone. Demon found himself squeezing through a space unfit for humans, forcing himself down and down, as if he were transgressing the outer boundaries of Hell itself. A small trickle of water flowed beneath him as the tunnel shrank even further and he was forced to push himself along on his back. Demon's gut rumbled with fear when he realized that he was pushing along blindly and could no longer see what was ahead.

The cold hard ceiling was now a mere two or three feet from his face. And soon the frightened squeals and squeaks of startled bats assailed his ears. He cried out when a small contingent of the winged mammals scurried from their roost, over his face, and back down the tunnel behind him. Demon fought down the revulsion and panic when one of the small bats latched onto his mask and screeched as the luchador thrashed back and forth in an effort to unseat the small beast. But a sense of relief came when the creature hopped over his lips and darted away into the darkness. Demon spat. "*Dios mío, man!*"

The anxious luchador inched his way through the remainder of the tunnel and came out on the far side. Once again, the cave opened up into a larger chamber, full of silent wonder. More stalactites and stalagmites rose from the floor and hovered on the ceiling, giving the cave the aura of the fantastic. If this was another time…another cave…he would bring his easel and paints down here and preserve this aesthetic vision on his canvas for posterity. Demon smiled. Not many fans knew that this massive bear of a wrestler was also an artist. Wouldn't *that* shock his adoring public?

A reddish tinge danced on the formations when they appeared in his flashlight beam, and Demon found himself spellbound once again at the natural wonder of this place. But he had no time for sightseeing. He took one more step, then froze.

Something moved ahead.

A shadow appeared along the wall, then vanished. Something *alive* was in this chamber, watching him from behind a large rock. He could feel its eyes on him, observing his every move. There would be no stealthy advance. They knew he was coming!

Demon moved closer. His voice echoed across the chamber. "I see you! Show yourself!"

Pure terror was not an emotion Red Demon experienced as a rule, but when the slimy, creeping thing emerged from behind the rock and the luchador beheld its gleaming eyes, bug-like fanged lips, and pinkish-white skin for the first time, he felt a stark fear rising from deep within himself that required every ounce of stamina and strength to fight back down.

The pitiful creature shielded its eyes from Demon's flashlight and the luchador was savvy enough to keep the beam right in the thing's face as a precaution against the potential threat. Obviously, the beast was not accustomed to such a harsh light. For now, this simple battery-operated torch would be Demon's bargaining chip.

The thing's voice was strained, as if it did not speak often. The sound of its words was a gruesome melody that whistled from its tiny mouth, "*Who…are…you, stranger? What do you…want here?*"

Demon pointed the light right into the thing's eyes and it fell back. "They call me Red Demon…"

The thing shielded its eyes with a short, suctioned arm and moved a step closer again. "*You have come for the girl?*"

Demon continued to hold the beast at bay with the light as he spoke. He silently prayed that the batteries held out. "Yes. Where is she?"

"*She is safe. You, however,…are not! Leave our home…go back to the upper world!*"

"Not without the girl!"

Before Red Demon could make a move, he was surrounded. The flashlight was knocked from his grip and taken from him. A dozen or more of the weird creatures descended upon him with tentacled arms sliding around his bare chest and arms, leaving a coating of slime that smelled of rot and decay and other terrible and unnamable things that lurked hidden beneath the earth that men walked upon. Even though the creatures moved slowly as individuals, as a team, their speed was blinding. They reminded Demon of an octopus he met once while diving off the coast of Acapulco. Long, suctioned tentacles shot from beneath the coral that day to grapple an unwary fish and pull it to its demise in the salty deep. Now, Demon was the fish and he was being pulled deeper into the caverns to face his own brand of destruction.

But he would not go without a brawl!

His fist struck the thing closest him and vanished into the monster's jelly-like flesh. The creature moaned and temporarily released his arm. Falling to the stone floor, Demon flipped another creature over his head. The humanoid worm sailed helplessly through the air and splatted against the far wall. The beast's slime oozed down the stone behind it and came to rest in a clear puddle. But before Demon could move again, a sharp, blinding pain shot through his shoulder. He glanced around just in time to see one of the worm-like creatures, with its beady eyes glowing a bright fluorescent yellow and its sharp ivory fangs embedded in his flesh.

The venom that pumped into his blood worked fast.

****

Red Demon awoke sometime later.

At first, he did not remember his whereabouts. But slowly, the venom began to wear off and the cave came into focus, as did his memory. He recalled why he now found himself in the soft semi-darkness of this subterranean world. *Ana.* He glanced around, but she was nowhere to be found. A soft, translucent light permeated the chamber, allowing him to see. The light was in no way bright, but it drenched everything in a dim illumination so that he was not lost in total darkness. He was thankful for that much. Some of the light came from strange, flameless torches that appeared to be glued to the wall with some kind of adhesive substance. These torches produced a white-blue glow. The worms themselves also put out a dim light. Their bodies glowed softly in the cave, making them perceptible to Demon's eyes.

Red Demon's mind throbbed and resonated with a strange haze and his body ached terribly, as if he had taken a beating unsurpassed in the ring. Gradually, he realized that he was lying on his back, chained to a stone slab.

A throng of the worm-things surrounded him. Red Demon groaned at the horror of their physical appearance. The things were disgusting to look at, but the luchador could not turn away. He lay there, a captive restrained, locked in the beady glare of the creatures' dark bulbous eyes.

They were not tall…perhaps a good four foot in height. They were almost albino, with the exception of a pinkish tinge that permeated their slimy flesh. Their bodies were completely hairless. A row of perhaps three short, stubby arms lined their chests. These members were suctioned, almost like the arms of a squid. They had no legs, only two similar, but larger, appendages like the arms. They rolled across the cave floor on these, leaving a revolting trail of slime in their wake.

One of them slithered closer and began to speak. "*You should not have come here.*"

Demon laughed. "*Sí* …tell me about it!"

"*The girl will not go with you. She has a higher purpose. With her help, we will gain the all-powerful tome that will give to us the supreme power on earth.*"

"The Necronomicon?"

The worm-thing took a step back and stared in shock at the chained wrestler. "*You know of this text?*"

"I can *read*, man! Yes, I know of this text. It should have been thrown on a fire ages ago!"

The creature snarled. "*You are a fool! We will gain control of The Necronomicon and with it, we will call down the omnipotent Cthulhu from the stars! We will open up the gates of hell and unleash all the demons to rain endless blood down on your world! We will unlock the dark secrets of the crawling things and they will rise from the tombs and swamps of the world to take their rightful place beside us!*"

The thing paused and a cruel smile broke across its face. Red Demon winced as a row of fangs protruded from its lower lip. *"We will give voice to the rats in the walls and conjure up Gol-Goroth and Bal-Sagoth to make mankind fall to its knees in fear! Finally, the worm men shall ascend to the upper world and rule as we have been destined to do for untold ages!"*

"That's quite a plan, amigo….but you forgot one thing," Red Demon said with a sneer.

"What is that?"

"You still have to get past me!"

The chamber burst out into wild laughter. All around him, the worm creatures cackled and howled. Red Demon looked around and smiled. "Laugh it up! When I get my chance, I am gonna break you all into greasy pieces!"

They looked so pathetic with their bellies wobbling and their slimy bodies contorting with laughter. But despite physical appearances, they were a race of monsters not to be underestimated. These weird beings had a plan for world domination, and unless Demon intervened, they just might pull it off.

It was fantastic. These monsters had lived far beneath the earth for eons, unknown to humans. Had they once ruled the upper world? Had mankind banished them to the caverns and pits of the earth's dark center? Perhaps they had once walked beneath the stars millennia before mankind was a blur in the eye of the cosmos. Perhaps they had ruled alongside the horrible god Cthulhu and vanished into the earth's core when their god returned to the stars with a half-whispered oath to return one day and conquer what was once his…

Red Demon's brain boggled at the unreal possibilities. There was little wonder that men went mad with knowledge such as this and spent their final days laughing uncontrollably in a padded room. And at the center of all this madness was *the book*. That damnable book. These things could never get control of The Necronomicon. Whatever the cost, he could not allow it.

Demon strained against his chains and his heart raced with adrenaline when he felt one of the screws start to give way and pull from the soft stone. He pushed against his bonds with everything he had, flexing the well-developed muscles in his arms and chest until the screws pulled free. Demon wrapped one end of the chain around his fist and jumped from the slab, swinging the long length like a broad bladed axe. The end of the chain caught one of the worm men across the head and its face vanished in an explosion of broken teeth and slimy green gore. Red Demon swung the thick chain again and another monster went down in a sickening pile of ooze and slime.

Demon kicked out and knocked two more to the stone floor, then he flipped himself over the heads of the advancing worm men and, using both hands, pulled the chain taut around the torsos of at least four of the vile creatures. With his biceps bulging, the luchador squeezed the chain until it cut through the worm bodies and unleashed a shower of black gut and yellow slime that reminded Demon of a squashed caterpillar.

One of the creatures screamed, "*Stop him!*"

But Red Demon would not be stopped so easily. His fist caught the beast and knocked it flat. Then he brought his boot heel down hard on the thing's cranium and grimaced with revulsion as its bloody brains exploded all over his red tights. Demon kicked the gory carcass away from him and leaped across the slab as the beasts came around the side after him. He kicked and punched his way through them and headed for the opening into the adjoining chamber where he stopped in his tracks and stared straight ahead in shock.

****

It was Ana, sitting on a stone seat, against the wall. But something was wrong with her. She sat like a silent angel in the dull glare of the cave light. She stared straight ahead and did not move or speak. She did not acknowledge Demon's presence in the least.

He flipped a worm man over his shoulder and drove his fist into the thing's face. Several more rushed into the chamber where Demon stood, but they all stopped and stared in awe at the silent girl.

"*You cannot take her*," one of the beasts screamed!

Demon glanced down at the base of Ana's throne. His flashlight lay beside her sandaled foot, as if it had been placed there as an offering by creatures who did not fully fathom what the device was actually used for. He reached down and grabbed the light, flicking on the switch and swinging a swath of light around, right into the eyes of the subterranean monsters behind him. Luckily the batteries were still good. The beam of light cut into the worm creatures like a sword blade and they scattered to the far corners of the chamber.

Demon grabbed the girl and pulled her towards him. "Let's go!" He carried her out of the chamber and back to the narrow tunnel, where she finally awoke from her trance and began to struggle. *"Put me down!"*

Red Demon did as she asked.

"There's a better way out of here," she said, coming to her senses. "Follow me!"

The girl led Demon back the opposite way, down a side passage that he never knew was there. The new tunnel led away from the main chamber and vanished into darkness before opening up again into another dimly lit room. And there in the midst of the ghostly blue light was a strange machine; cold blue metal of some otherworldly alloy…reaching to the roof of the cavern. A solid ton of metal rushed downwards, forming a long cylindrical cannon, the very tip of which was as slender as a man's thumb. It pointed to a spot on the floor. The device was unlike any earthly machinery Red Demon had ever seen.

"Anna…what is this? What do these monsters use this infernal machine for?"

The girl stared in awe at the great machine. "This is a growth ray. They use this machine to make monsters."

"What kind of monsters?"

The ear-piercing sound of a laser filled the chamber. Demon rushed over to the control panel, but there was no one operating it. Some unseen force moved the lever and pressed the buttons that brought the alien craftsmanship to life. An ominous red button glowed and pulsated as the laser expanded and began to move. The cannon itself moved automatically, cutting a trench into the very rock of the cave floor. There was a commotion, as if the darkness down in the shallow trench was moving. Demon gasped as dozens of crawling things squirmed up from beneath the floor, finally free. The writhing, quivering army of insects and arachnids were devoid of any color and shined an almost solid white in the glare of the laser, which drenched their hides in a crimson hue of unknown properties, but strangely enough did not kill them. Instead, the red light of the laser had the opposite effect. It nourished the creeping bodies and made them grow in size! Demon stood there, transfixed with horror as cockroaches, centipedes, and spiders grew to the size of a small dog…then to the size of a human being and beyond! In a span of mere seconds, Red Demon found himself cowering beneath the towering might of super insects that rose from the cavern floor and hovered over Demon and Ana with mandibles dripping saliva and claws that sliced the air and reached out ravenously for prey.

The insects were blind. The heads were devoid of eyes. This was not an uncommon trait in subterranean insects that frequented the deeper confines of caves. But this fact did not make the giant creatures less deadly. In fact, much to Demon's chagrin, it gave the things an almost supernatural ability to hear and sense.

Ana backed towards the cavern's exit, with her eyes locked upon the clicking horrors that glared down at the two helpless humans. Demon could hear her labored breathing as she tried to escape. A cockroach, as big now as a three-story building stepped from the ray and advanced towards the terrified girl.

"Careful," Demon whispered. "Don't move…those things can't see, but they can hear your heartbeat!" The girl began to cry uncontrollably, and the sound caused the giant roach's antennae to wriggle and search. Its mandibles snapped open and shut in anticipation of her succulent flesh. Red Demon reached out to Ana as she moved past but the girl broke free and raced in panic for the exit, which may have well been a million miles away.

The cockroach lunged hungrily after the girl, but before it could wrap its pincers around her, a humongous spider bounced out of nowhere and snatched Ana up in its mouth! She screamed as the horrible white arachnid scurried up the wall and across the ceiling with its juicy prize already vanishing in a web cocoon.

Demon cried out in terror. He sprinted after them, but the roach, satisfied with a consolation prize, grappled Demon with its razor pincers. The luchador was at the savage mercy of the creature as it lifted him skyward. Trickles of warm blood rose to the surface of Demon's skin and rolled down his chest. The smell of blood made the monster crazy and it roared savagely. The sound was deafening. Demon's ears rang and he fought to maintain consciousness as the roach squeezed tighter. In a second, he would be devoured. Ana would die also, and the worms would move forward with their plan of world domination. It was not only the prospect of death that Red Demon faced, but also the utter defeat of mankind. And there was nothing he could do about it.

He was going to die…far beneath the surface of the earth. The Necronomicon would fall into the hands of evil beings and the Elder Gods would return. Red Demon's eyes misted over beneath his mask as the sounds of the ring escorted him into the next life. It was crazy, but he could feel the mat and taste the salt of his own sweat. He could hear the bell ring and more than that, he could hear the roar of the crowd as they cheered for him and chanted his name on Saturday nights long past.

Demon cried out. His life could not end this way. The world could not end this way. He kicked and screamed as the slavering mouth of the giant insect loomed closer and closer. The creature was straight out of a nightmare or a really bad B-movie; the kind that languished in the run-down sections of Mexican towns in old half-condemned theatres that boasted big rats, broken seats, and sticky floors. The kind of flicks that ran and ran until the film stock deteriorated into scratched, cigarette burned celluloid scar tissue that would hardly endure the thousandth indignity of being fed through a projector once again and not for the last time.

He could feel the monster's hot breath on his face now. He could feel the moisture of its saliva and see the black pit of its gullet as he was raised higher and higher into the fiend's mouth. A horrible clicking sound filled his ears and brain as Red Demon closed his eyes for the last time. Somewhere, far away in the back regions of his mind came the warm applause from a full house for a match well fought.

****

The giant roach shook violently, and the next thing Red Demon knew he was falling through space. The cold hard cavern floor came rushing up to meet him and he landed on his back and rolled, coming to a stop against the side of the worm men's diabolical machinery. The ray was still burning a crevice in the stone floor, still creating giants to rend and tear. A roar echoed across the cavern. A fight for the ages was happening over Demon's aching head. The source of his salvation was even now battling it out with the flesh-eating roach for some primitive supremacy beneath the earth: a writhing centipede as big as a locomotive. The creature hissed and slithered about, wrapping its segmented body around the roach's midsection and squeezing the life from its foe. Gobs of yellow blood formed around the roach's mouth and the crunching sound of its breaking exo-skeleton signaled the finish. The centipede let the dead giant drop from its grasp and immediately turned on a large arachnid hovering nearby.

Demon picked himself up and struggled to regain his breath. Nothing appeared broken; however, there was little doubt that he would feel the pain later. The centipede and its new arachnid foe were too preoccupied to notice Demon escaping, but the other insects were only just realizing that a meal was at hand and not one of them wanted to share. As soon as the colossal monsters smelled Demon's blood and heard the steady rhythm of his heartbeat, they lunged. Two bone white spiders, with round bellies and long pencil thin legs, shot webbing at the running luchador, but he managed to dive and roll. He sprang back to his feet and headed for the laser. Just as the spiders descended upon him, Demon swung the laser cannon skyward and severed a large stalactite, hanging from the roof above like an icicle. The broken rock came crashing downward, smashing the cannon and crushing the bloodthirsty spiders into mush. The other insects scurried away but resumed their fight to the death immediately. Demon exited the chamber with its hissing horrors and found his way into the adjoining room where the great spider had carried Ana.

"Please don't let me be too late," Red Demon prayed as he bounced over a large boulder with his glittering cape flying behind him. There, against the wall, was Ana, struggling against the thick webbing that held her tight. The spider had begun a larger web that reached the ceiling above and the far walls on each side. Demon stopped and slowly navigated his way through the room, taking care not to become entangled in the great arachnid's web. "Ana! I am here! Hang on!"

The girl turned her head and a smile of relief broke across her beautiful face. "Red Demon! Help me!"

Demon crawled beneath part of the web and reached Ana. He took a knife from his boot and sawed through the strands that bound the girl until they gave way. Then they headed for the far tunnel that led to the upper world and freedom. But the spider returned, hungrier than ever, and angry over the theft of its hard-earned food.

It sprang, knocking demon to the floor. Before he could react, the oversized arachnid was on him, with fangs bared and dripping with venom. The spider's enormous weight held Demon to the ground as it leaned in for the kill.

One kiss, and Demon was through. But Red Demon was not going to surrender…not yet. He had come too far. The luchador shoved his knife deep into the creature's abdomen and twisted the blade, opening up a large wound that bled gallons of slime and blood. The sickening gore rolled down Demon's arm and covered his chest. The arachnid gyrated and convulsed in its death throes then slumped over, quite dead. Red Demon crawled out from under the terrible spider and pulled Ana along with him to the waiting tunnel.

But the worm men were not through with Red Demon! A half dozen of the slimy creatures rushed him. Ana screamed and ran from their clutches. One of the worms howled, *"Get her! Do not let her escape!"*

Demon kicked a worm-thing in the chest and knocked it down, then he pile-drived another and smashed in the face of yet another. The piercing pain of fangs ripping into his flesh caused Demon to pause, but he did not stop. He lashed out and punched the worm, then flipped it over his head and into the oncoming rush of other worms.

Demon launched himself into the air, caught a worm with his ankles and sent the beast crashing to the floor. Its brains left a green puddle that grew larger by the second. Demon stepped over the mess and took another worm down. He fought the dizziness away. Luckily, the creature wasn't able to inject as much venom into his body this time.

He shouted to the girl, "Come on! Keep moving!"

Two more worms appeared from the darkness and desperately attempted to stop the prisoners from escaping. Demon was too strong, too fast. He stiff armed the next worm and vaulted over another, pulling Ana along. Soon the two of them were racing down the dark tunnel, en route to freedom!

Red Demon shivered when he realized that his flashlight was gone. There was a lot of tunnel to transverse before they were safe, and the endless possibilities they could encounter in the dark filled him with dread. "I lost the light, Ana. Making our way back to the surface won't be easy," Demon muttered.

Ana glanced behind them. Demon could hear the distant hissing of the worms as they gave chase. "They come. We must go," Ana said in an emotionless, monotone voice. She took Red Demon by the hand and led him through the tunnel and back through the caverns.

Demon could hear the worms scurrying in the darkness behind them. He could hear them whispering and calling to one another. "*Hurry! Catch them! She cannot escape!*" Ana seemed unfazed by the pursuers. She pulled the weary luchador along with her and eventually they reached the outer opening of the cave. The worms fell back at some point, when the outer world was in sight and their frantic whisperings faded away into the night.

The moon had descended in the sky by the time Red Demon and Ana left the cave. Demon fell to his knees and breathed a long sigh of relief. *"¡Gracias a Dios!* I began to think we would never see the stars again!" He glanced up at Ana. She stood there, staring upwards at the firmament, as if searching for something.

"Ana? Are you alright?"

The girl glanced at Demon as if she had been waked from a dream. "What? Oh…yes. I am fine. Come…take me to my father."

****

Red Demon's convertible pulled up at Dr. Huerta's ranch house. The stars swirled above, still hiding secrets and worlds unknown to man. The night held its secrets, too, and

Demon had much to learn still. He helped Ana from the car and escorted her to the front door.

The old man opened the door with a relieved look on his face and threw his arms around his daughter. He sobbed with joy and held the girl to him. Then he brought her in and shook Demon's hand repeatedly, thanking him before finally inviting him inside.

"Let me make you some coffee, my boy! It is the least I can do for the man who rescued my daughter and saved the world…"

Red Demon laughed. "If it is all the same with you, Doctor…I am going home to take a shower and collapse into my bed. I have brought your daughter back. Take the Necronomicon and burn it. Tonight. Take no more chances. Next time I may not be able to help. Buenas noches."

"Buenas Noches, Red Demon. I will do as you ask…and thank you again!"

Demon waved and hopped into his convertible and in a flash, the masked wrestler was speeding back across the mountain to his bungalow in the valley.

****

Something woke Dr. Huerta sometime later. It was still dark and the house was cold with that pre-dawn chill that always crept up the valley just before sunrise. He sat up in bed and tried to shake the grogginess from his brain. The clock was ticking somewhere in the darkness. His heart jumped when he heard the noise again…the sound that obviously woke him.

Someone was in the study!

His blood turned cold suddenly. The Necronomicon…it was locked in the safe. Were they *here*…in his house…to steal the damnable book after their kidnapping plot failed? The old man rose and took the pistol from his nightstand. He checked to make sure it was still loaded and made his way through the bedroom, and down the shadow choked hall.

Dr. Huerta stopped in front of the study.

A crash made him jump. Someone was in there. He took a deep breath and reached inside the study, flipping on the lights. The old man rushed in with his gun raised. His jaw dropped. Standing there, before him, was Ana. She held The Necronomicon in her hands. Huerta glanced behind her. The wall safe was hanging open.

The old man's heart sank. "Ana…no…please tell me it isn't so!"

"I am afraid it is, Father," the girl said in a monotone voice. "I am taking The Necronomicon and you will not stop me."

"And you will take it to those creatures in the cave?"

The girl's voice changed. She hissed, sending cold chills down Dr. Huerta's spine. "*Enough! Get out of my way, old man!*" Ana's face became a blur momentarily and then began to change. Huerta watched in utter shock as his daughter's eyes turned into dark orbs and her face melted into the terrible visage of the conquering worm!

Dr. Huerta screamed, but his horror was interrupted when Red Demon burst into the room. "*Demon*! Where did you come from?"

"I waited around, Dr. Huerta…something about Ana didn't seem right. All the emotion is gone from her and I couldn't help but note that back in the caves, she could actually see in the dark."

Huerta looked mournfully at the creature who was once his daughter. "Oh, Ana! My poor child! It would appear that Red Demon is right!" The old man turned to Demon. "What do we do now?"

Red Demon reached into his belt and produced a vial. "It occurred to me while I was deep in the caves. What is the one thing that will kill a slug?"

Huerta thought for a moment. "*Salt?*"

"Exactly. If only I had carried some with me into the caverns." Demon shot a sympathetic glance at the old man. "I am sorry, Professor. But this must be done." Huerta looked away and nodded. Demon tossed the contents of the vial over Ana's face. The room was filled with a gut-wrenching howl of pain and in seconds, Ana was dead on the floor, melting into a putrid pile!

Red Demon studied the dead creature on the floor and started to remove his mask. Dr. Huerta grabbed his arm and stopped him. "No, Red Demon. Stop. Why are you unmasking yourself?"

"I…I am retiring after this night."

"But you did not lose."

"I killed your only daughter, Doctor. I am giving up my life as a luchador."

"No, my son. I will not let you. You saved the world from destruction. With that book, the worm men would have summoned up all the horrors of the cosmos to conquer and destroy."

"But I could not save your daughter…"

"No one could, my boy. Go now…in peace…and fight another day. We are depending on you."

Red Demon thought for a moment and fastened his mask again. "Yes, Professor."

"Here, Red Demon…take The Necronomicon with you! Destroy it!" Huerta reached for the book. The old man paused and a look of terror came over his face.

"Professor," Red Demon said. "What's wrong?"

"The Necronomicon…it's *gone*…"

"The Man at the End of the World"

There's this man I want to tell you about…this carny dwarf named Carlo.

I knew him back in 1932, and he has haunted my memories and dreams ever since. He was an outcast, like me, and he knew secrets and traveled to strange worlds unknown to most mortals. His daylight world was the carnival but deep in the night, when nobody was around, he put on a different hat.

He became something bigger and more fantastic than anything you could ever imagine.

Carlo revolved around the big people's world his whole life, but none of them really knew him. Most never wanted to know him. He spent years cleaning up the carnival grounds, and carting trunks and boxes. He cared for the horses. He performed under the big tent, acting the clown for the entertainment of the masses. He ran out there, under the lights every night with a million-watt smile plastered across his little face.

But inside he was lacerated and bleeding.

He endured all the laughter and praise as if it were all the same bullets. Nobody really knows where he came from. Carlo just showed up one day and asked where the boss was. Sir Richard was the kind of carny boss every freak dreams of. He didn't judge, and he didn't make any distinction between the deformed, the beaten down, and the world of The Normals. In fact, he liked being around his people, the carnival folk, more than anyone considered *normal* by outside society.

You have to understand our world. We were the outcasts. The unwanted. The freaks and deviants of the world, with no place else to turn. You learn how to juggle fire, or to contort yourself into a pretzel. You learn how to swallow swords or roll your eyes back inside your skull. You learn how to bite the heads off live chickens or play a violin with your feet. In a lot of ways that becomes your pride, your fulfillment.

All of us have at least one great gift: I weigh 70 pounds and look like a walking skeleton. Beth, the fat lady weighs over 400 pounds and looks like an elephant dancing through the night. The bird man has the IQ of a toad, but he's a real sweetheart, and can sing all of Stephen Foster's songs. He just doesn't know what any of the words mean. The clowns, the lion tamer, the snake charmers and fire eaters. The Pin Man. The Iguana Boy. The Siamese Sisters. We all have a home in the carnival. A slot in the universe.

Everyplace else is just a myth.

But Carlo…he was special, and he had gifts that none of us had. He had gifts that none of us really even understand yet.

I'll admit that I didn't see anything to whoop and holler about when he first came to work with us. He was just a little guy that never said much. But we all accepted him right away and made him a part of our society. It's just that he didn't seem to make any steps towards us. But that's alright. Like I said, you have to understand us. Our kind endures a lot of pain just to remain among the living…and when a man doesn't want to talk, we all respect that.

But that didn't tame our curiosity. The Fat Lady stopped by my tent very often on the way back from the night's performance to ask if I had spoken to the new guy. And the first few hundred times she asked me that, I hadn't.

But one afternoon…maybe it was in October…Carlo dropped by and, of course, I invited him in. I made a pot of fresh tea while my thoughts rushed forward and bumped into each other. We sat there a few minutes, not saying much, and exchanging nods and smiles. Then he asked me how long I had been a carnival man. The first thing I noticed was the sound of his voice. It was a weary voice, strained, as if he had traveled a million long miles just to sit in my tent and drink tea.

His voice sounded as if all he wanted in the world was to rest. Just rest. Like he had some great burden he couldn't lay down.

I never forgot that first conversation we had. Of course, it wasn't much of a conversation, but I learned a little about him. And I began to really like him.

Sometimes at night, when I couldn't sleep and felt like a walk, I would stop by Carlo's tent to see if he was sleeping. Once he walked along with me for a spell. But other nights there was a lantern burning softly inside and he was gone.

****

At some point I began to notice the deaths occurring in the towns we passed through. Mostly the elderly, but sometimes it was the sick or terminally ill children. It was almost as if some force, benign or not, was putting them out of their miseries. Passing more and more funeral processions on our way out of town became a regularity. People dressed in black. Wagons carrying the dead to their final resting places. At the time, I didn't think much of it. People die every day.

Carlo's weariness grew. Like a fungus with every funeral procession we passed. Every fresh grave that waited in the local cemetery. Every obituary in the newspapers that we devoured hungrily on our way through this too big world that we found ourselves in.

But life rolled on in the carnival, like the wagon wheels beneath us. Life has a habit of doin' that. It never stops. For nobody.

It wasn't long before Carlo began to drop by my tent on a regular basis. I would be standing over the wash basin, rinsing my handsome face and I would hear, "*Harv?*"

I let him call me Harv. Everyone else does. I would always dress quickly, and we would walk over to the Bearded Lady's tent for a cup of coffee. Her name was Heloise, and let me tell you, if you could get past the fact that she had a finer damned beard than your grandpa, she was quite a looker. And she made *one hell* of a cup of coffee.

But it wasn't the Bearded Lady that stole Carlo's heart…it was the Fire Eater's wife. And therein lies the tragedy.

****

The Fire Eater had no name that I know of. He was just *The Fire Eater*. The crowds went wild when he shoved a flaming poker down his gullet. He was one of the main attractions, actually. He was from some far-off country in the East, maybe India. Hell, he could've been a used car dealer from Jersey for all I knew. He was olive skinned and wore a turban. He kept a beard and carried a long-curved sword like them Arabian Knights useta carry. So what?

But what I did know, was that he was one *mean son of a bitch*. Everyone stayed out of his way. I mean everyone…even the boss. The guy made everybody as nervous as a pimply faced boy in a cathouse. He was thin, but all muscles, and Jean, his beautiful blue-eyed blonde wife, was his *property*, his object, and anyone that dared as much as a glance at her sideways got his face caved in.

The Fire Eater swallowed fire like most men swallowed gin, and he could slice the air into loaves with his blade that he kept sharpened into a fine razor edge. The rubes screamed and applauded every time he went to twirling that damned sword. He could spin the blade so fast that you would never even see it. And he never cut himself with it, more's the pity. If I thought that God had made him for one second, I would say that God never made a meaner bastard. But I ain't so sure that God made him. All I know is that he ruled Jean with an iron claw. And man, when he said *jump,* she *jumped.*

Well, things being what they were, Carlo took to Jean right away, and she took to him. I mean…she being a big person, it wasn't that she loved him like *that*…even though he loved her that way. It was obvious enough. It was that she could *talk* to him. And he *listened.* They told each other their secrets. But only if she got The Fire Eater drunk first, or if he was performing and she knew he would be gone for an hour or so.

The problem was that she wanted to talk to Carlo more and more. She had found someone who appreciated her soul and not the fact that she looked like a brand-new kewpie doll; and she liked unburdening her heart to Carlo. She trusted him. So she was getting her husband drunker and drunker, and it was beginning to take its toll on the bastard. The last performance he gave was when he slipped and burnt his face. Ruined his good looks. And who do you think he blamed?

I'll never forget that night.

The Fire Eater stormed into his tent after scorching his face in front of a thousand paying customers. He got there earlier than usual, and Jean was gone. He marched through the camp, howling like a demon and breaking everything that crossed his path. He knocked The Bird Boy down into the dust and walked right over his back. I was scared, but I was angry. I almost went after him, but Heloise pulled me back.

His screams were filled with the most devilish rage you ever heard, and with agony, too. Everyone prayed right away that he didn't find Carlo with his wife. We knew something bad was going to happen.

The Fire Eater grabbed every freak he could lay his hands on, so mad that his words melted into a garbled dead language that nobody could understand anymore. He threw the Iguana Boy across his tent and ripped it down over his wobbling head. He smacked the Bearded Lady, knocked her to the ground, and that's when I stepped in. I couldn't stay out of it any longer.

I may be thin as a rail, but I hit him in the face as hard as I could. And then the next thing I know I am flying through the air and everything goes black. When I came to, I felt the Bearded Lady's tears falling on my face like rain drops.

I couldn't move or speak. I just lay there watching her cry over me. And it seemed the entire camp was crying. People hugged each other and wailed. Sir Richard kept shaking his head and saying over and over, *"It's awful. It's awful."*

The Fire Eater had *killed* Jean. Strangled her out in the field behind the camp. Carlo tried to stop him, but he's only three feet high. He just got knocked away like a little fly.

He ran back to get help, but it was too late.

I didn't talk to Carlo for a few days. I figure that a man is entitled to his own private grief. They took The Fire Eater away. We never saw him again.

Probably hung him.

I sure as hell hope they did.

****

The carnival moved on to the next town. That's the beauty of carnival life. There are a million and one bright eyed and bushy-tailed tomorrows just waiting to come to you and reveal their treasures. It's the kind of living that makes you want to believe in sunrise, and we all did. The troublesome night in one town quickly vanished into a fresh day at the next. And we were happily washed along with the current.

I waited a day or two, then went over to Carlo's tent. The first time was at night, but he wasn't there. I don't know where he went; I mean where can you go? I guess he walked into town, and I worried for him. Freaks should stick to their own kind. It's safest.

Each night, after Jean's murder, was the same. Carlo vanished. I finally caught a glimpse of him, though. Watering the horses. And the following morning, he spoke to me. It was if I had been asleep and his words woke me. I was happy to talk with my friend again. But now he was different. His soul dragged the ground. You could tell he had lost something he knew he would never find again.

Who knows what Jean and Carlo talked about all those hours? They shared something most people, Normal or Freak, will never have.

The sweetest things between a man and a woman aren't always of the body, and I think that these two shared a common something that only the mind and heart know. And to be frankly honest, I was jealous. I was jealous because Carlo had found something I never found. But that jealousy turned to pity real quick, because the saddest thing is to see someone with something more than special, and to then have to watch them lose it and suffer through a thousand deep dark nights without it. Holding only the knowledge that they once had it in their hands but couldn't keep it. That's worse than never having it at all.

It was late one night, around midnight, that these thoughts were plaguing me but good. I could no more catch a wink of sleep than the man in the moon could, and I felt like the thing to cure my wakefulness was a visit to Carlo's tent. I didn't know if he would be awake or not, but I was gambling that he would be.

If you have never walked through a carnival camp at night, you have missed a picture of life that you will never see anywhere else. Because a carnival is its own culture. Its own society, with all the wonderment and love that a people can muster.

There is beauty in the wagons. There is beauty in the waddling grunts of the deformed and unwanted spirits and the way they laugh with each other and depend on each other. There is a beauty in the dawn. There is a beauty in the dusk. And in the stew pot bubbling in the evening chill. There is a beauty in the sad longing we all feel in the darkness alone in our tents. The Normals never see this.

Dozens of tents set up on either side of a dirt road, trampled and worn down by miles of wagon wheel and horse hoof, all arriving late at night to set up a new world for The Normals to experience. A new world that they can stare at, and laugh at, and point at. But we just give them what they want. We dance and sing and make ourselves into clowns or savages. We swallow swords and fire. Swing through the air like exotic angels. Flip and twist and bounce. Squawk and crow and howl like beasts.

We become what they fear inside themselves.

And above this world of ours is the *real* tent top. The *supreme* big top. The firmament stitched together with the darkest of silks. Poked full of shining holes that the angels peek through and smile. This covers and warms us all, and somehow we go to sleep at night peacefully in the immense vision of it all.

I was walking along, through the sleeping camp; the lights slowly snuffing out and the darkness gathering around all the tents and wagons slowly and peacefully. I heard the laughter bouncing from tent to tent and felt the breeze winding through, navigating around the sleepers like soft fingers reaching for children with dreams.

I saw light coming from Carlo's tent when I got there. He was still up and I found myself happy with the prospect of talking to him.

"I was expecting you," he said when I stuck my head through the tent flap. In my hurry to see my friend I forgot my manners and forgot to call to him first, which was the custom.

"Expecting me? What for?"

Carlo turned around to look at me. His face was an ancient mask of nerves. Before either of us could speak again, I saw why.

Sitting in a chair opposite from Carlo was *Jean*!

****

My jaw dropped. Jean just sat there. It was her alright, but she looked like an image in a smoky mirror. You could almost see through her.

"What…in God's name…?"

Carlo shrugged. "I shouldn't have done it."

I replied, but never took my eyes off Jean's specter. *"Done what?"*

It was almost as if Jean wasn't there. She said nothing and acted as if she was the only one in the tent. She stared off into space and her transparent body pulsated. She had this weird glow about her like she was hooked up to an electric light.

She gazed off into a world we couldn't see.

Carlo's voice cracked as he spoke. "I stole Jean back from the underworld."

I was completely ice-cold stunned for a couple of minutes, but I found the ability to speak again. "How…how the hell did you do…*that*?" A chill danced on the back of my neck. I began to shiver, and wanted to run away, but I couldn't force my legs to move an inch.

Carlo stared longingly at Jean. He acted like he wasn't sure if he should say more, but he finally confided in me. "I bring souls to their final reward. I show them the way. It's what I do."

I tried to break the thick anxious air, but it was half-hearted on my part. "You can't just buy them a bus ticket?"

Carlo didn't laugh. He kept staring at the ghostly image in front of him as tears welled up in his eyes. *"I shouldn't have done it."*

I pulled a stool up beside him and sat. For a small eternity the two of us sat there and stared at Jean. Carlo was numb. He truly did not know what to do.

After a few minutes I tried to speak to her. "Jean," I called to her. "Jean." After three times, she responded, but she never looked at me. She continued to look off into an eternity I could only guess at.

"I am tired," she moaned. *"So tired. Let me rest."* Her voice sounded as if she were speaking from the bottom of the ocean.

Carlo buried his head in his hands. "She doesn't do anything but sit there and say over and over, *I'm tired.*"

The obvious question came like a thunderstorm. "What are you gonna do?"

"I don't know," he said. And I knew he really meant it.

I studied Carlo. He returned to the underworld to bring back the love of his life to the land of the living. He let his heart rule his mind. Once gone, a soul can never return and be the same. A soul needs a body. Or it is just a soul. I didn't know how I knew that, but somehow I did. Now he sat there, with a ghost, and he suffered all the agonies of the lovelorn. I wanted to help my friend, but there was nothing I could do. This was out of a Thin Man's realm of experience.

"Carlo." I tried to be delicate. "You should take her back."

He wheeled around and locked eyes with mine. "I *can't*. You don't know what it's like to live without her."

"You can't keep her, Carlo. She doesn't belong here anymore."

He began to cry. His little body heaved and convulsed. I could've died right along with him. Finally, he looked at me, "You're right. I have to take her back."

Carlo rose and wiped his face with a towel. He paused, then he motioned towards Jean and beckoned her. "Come, dear. Come along with me."

She rose slowly. "*I am tired*," she said to nobody in particular.

"I know. Come with me." He led her through the tent flap. I watched them go and the melancholy welled up deep from inside my gut. And then Carlo did the unexpected, as if I had expected any of this. He grabbed my arm, "*You come, too*."

****

I tried to protest. I mean it wasn't as if he was taking me to Cleveland. I had no idea where I was going, and it didn't sound like too peachy a place. But his grip on my arm was so strong, and he pulled me along with him so quickly that I could not find it in my constitution to pull away.

So we went.

We moved silently through the camp and into the dark fields beyond. There were no stars. The inky shadows and the chill wind swirled around us, and I swear it was as if we were being carried along by some unknown force.

Finally, we stopped. Time and distance was a mystery. We could have been out there for days and I wouldn't have noticed. We were in a big open field someplace. Directly before us was a flash of light, almost as if from lightning, but it didn't go away. It appeared, and it stayed until we stepped into it. Carlo pulled me and Jean into the light.

At first it was completely dark, but slowly my eyes began to adjust, and I began to see that we were in a huge cave. The ceiling hung low and I reached up to touch it. A clammy wetness coated my hand. Ahead of us was more darkness, but I could see perfectly well now, despite the fact. It was as if I was in the middle of a sea made of pure midnight, lost in the deep blueness of it.

My body felt so strange. I really felt nothing at all anymore. Not even fear. Jean walked ahead of me now, zombie-like and passive. Carlo was still leading her. Even though he had turned me loose, I still followed. Now I wanted to. I had to.

We walked along in silence, but at some point…when, I can't recall…there was sound all around us.

Swallowing us up. Indescribable sound, like a universe of voices all merged into a long, winding drone with trombones and tubas mixed in and playing very slow. It was the strangest noise ever heard by human ears.

And then came the light. It hurt my eyes at first, but then we were in the middle of it, standing in a large cavern. The walls were streaked with shadow, but now there was light, and I couldn't tell you where it came from.

We moved down a dusky side tunnel and I heard something. Some kind of beast lurked ahead, waiting for us. I could hear the thing snarling and scratching at the dirt. I could feel the heat from its rancid breath. We couldn't see it yet, but I knew it was big. It sounded like a vicious dog…or wolf.

All of a sudden there were two or three more of them just around the corner ahead, and they all growled in unison.

My feet froze in the sand and my blood curdled like old milk. "What is *that*, Carlo?"

The beasts howled just then and I nearly lost my skin!

Carlo stopped and glanced back at me with a nervous look on his face. "We can't stop here, my friend. Keep moving."

"Moving ahead…up there?"

"Yes. It'll be alright. Let's go."

I tried to have faith in my friend…but he was only three feet high in thick heeled boots with inserts, and that didn't give me much confidence in our collected ability to defend ourselves. But I shrugged and we moved ahead anyway.

More growls.

Whatever the thing was, it was warning us to stop. We rounded the curve and my stomach did a cartwheel up into my throat. Up ahead loomed the biggest damned wolf hound I've ever seen. *And it had three heads…*

The beast was *hu-normous*. Its dark fur bristled and its three heads, full of razor-sharp fangs, rolled around on its thick neck, growling and barking as the slobber bubbled and foamed on its black lips.

The thing took a few steps towards us. The deafening, enraged sound of its canine voices echoed off the walls and made me cover my ears. Suddenly I felt something again. I don't mind saying that I was petrified. I weighed less than a hundred pounds, but my skeletal frame would have still made a good chew toy.

"*Cerberus*," Carlo announced. "He's mad at me."

The thing certainly looked mad enough. I gulped and tried to speak. "Why?"

"I got one over on him." Carlo patted Jean on the arm. "I stole Jean out from under his nose. I'm probably the first." Jean still stared straight ahead at whatever awaited us on the other end of the tunnel.

Carlo approached the dog, which was clearly and viciously angry at him. "I'm sorry I did it. Please forgive me. I brought her back." The thing continued venting its anger at Carlo. I could see bits of spit glistening in the light and flying through the air. The dog's yellow fangs were getting very close to Carlo. Too close for comfort.

"Carlo…be careful!" I whispered.

"Let us pass," Carlo said. "I brought her back…I want to make things right again."

The three-headed dog took a step back and lowered its heads. But it never took its eyes away. And it kept growling; its voice a droning hum of threat and promise. The damned thing didn't know whether to let Carlo pass or not. You could see it thinking hard with all three brains.

"Let us pass," Carlo repeated soothingly. "You know me, boy. You know me." The beast stepped aside. It was unbelievable. It breathed in great agonized gulps of cave air as we passed.

We walked farther down the corridor. I could still hear the three-headed beast snorting and pawing at the sand behind us. "That thing back there," I asked. "That dog…I read about it once. He's the guardian of the underworld, right?"

"That's right."

"But that was back in them Greek days…"

"I've been around awhile, Harv."

"How long?"

"I'm old. Old as time. I remember that thing's three-headed great-grand daddy," Carlo said dryly. "I remember dawn on the Euphrates and sunsets on the Nile. I remember sea salt in my nostrils, the smell of storms on the top of jungle covered pyramids, and starlight shining on tombs so old that even the gods couldn't recall who was buried there. I remember waiting out ice storms in caves with painted walls and riding on riverboats down the Mississippi. I been around." I could tell he didn't really want to talk anymore about it, so we moved on in silence. But my mind was reeling like an out of control Ferris wheel.

Shadows continued to dance on the walls, and the light began to fade, but I wasn't scared anymore. We walked for a good ways until the tunnel ended and we emerged into a large open area. I couldn't tell if we were still in the caverns or if we had stepped out into a dark overcast night.

We walked on until the three of us came to the banks of a river. It wasn't big like the Mississippi, but it was bigger than a lot of the western rivers we traveled over during our carny days. A boatman waited there. He was tall and thin, and draped from head to toe in a long black robe, with a cowl that hid his face. He said nothing and moved real slow like he had all the time in the universe. I guess maybe he did. Carlo said something to him that I couldn't quite make out. It could have been in a different language for all I know. I heard Carlo call the boatman *Charon*.

We were about to step onboard when I heard a flurry of horse hooves and I wheeled around. My jaw dropped and I started babbling like an idiot. Looming over us was a horse man…the lower half of him was a horse, and the top half was a bare-chested man! He pulled the string back on a wicked looking bow and pointed a razor-sharp arrow in our direction as if he intended on using it.

And what's crazy is that the thing *spoke*. "You finally decided to come back, you little bastard?"

Carlo sighed. I could tell he had to handle this situation diplomatically or we were in big trouble. "Yes, Pholus…look, I'm real sorry for skipping out and stealing this soul. I brought her back."

I heard the bowstring creak as it stretched even further. "So?"

Carlo thought for a moment and reached into his pocket. He held out three large coins. "Here…will this make my apology more palatable?"

The centaur accepted the gift and studied the coins for a long moment, turning them round and round with his fingers. He finally smiled. "I suppose so. I can't stay mad at you long, Carlo. You can cross…go ahead."

Carlo helped Jean into the long boat, then held his hand out for me. I hesitated. "Come on," Carlo whispered, "we don't have to pay."

I climbed in and before I sat down in the boat, I got a good look at the boatman. My breath caught in my throat as I looked beneath his cowl. The boatman was *a living skeleton*…a death's head. On his bone white face was etched an eternal sardonic grin. He gazed at me through black eyeless sockets. My soul rolled over inside me at that point. I sat down without as much as another word and the haunted boatman poled us away from the rocky shore.

No one spoke as the boatman poled us across the dark river. The water on both sides of the craft was like obsidian. It swirled and the spray from the rapids wet my face and shirt. The water felt strange. I can't explain it. The drops on my flesh felt as if they were alive almost. I gazed down into the river and I couldn't even see my reflection at first. Then I could see perfectly well and I howled in fear as I saw a skeletal face peering back at me.

I fell back in the seat and Carlo put his hand on my shoulder. Almost immediately I calmed down. "Don't look into the water," he said.

There were great black rocks in the river and somehow the boatman poled us around all of them. The dark water began to rage more and more violently the farther along we went, pushing us closer towards the rocky outcrops along the far shore. The more the thought of our hides colliding with stone occurred to me, the more skillfully the boatman maneuvered us away from danger.

Large fish that resembled carp swam alongside the boat at one point. When I glanced down I saw that they had *human faces*! Faces that gazed longingly up at me, almost pleading with me. Their eyes sad and forlorn. And then, in an instant, the things vanished beneath the dark waters.

Carlo smiled awkwardly. "Those were the souls of the damned. Sometimes they become fish."

I just sat there and tried not to look at the water again.

The rapids were dream-like and tossed our boat about like a piece of kindling. I thought we would capsize, but somehow we didn't. The boatman was a master. I had never seen anything like it. And when we finally came through the raging section of the river, a mind shattering length of time where color and darkness and light competed for the brain and the eyes, it somehow felt as if it had never happened. Carlo sat next to Jean and held her hand the entire time.

Soon our voyage was over. We reached the far shore and there was such light. Everywhere. Bright and golden and pure. My eyes feasted…my heart felt like it would burst from my chest. I had never seen such beauty or felt such contentment in my soul.

Carlo helped Jean out of the boat. They walked away, into blue…and green…and red…an eternal summer of the mind. Into the flowery center of what we all wanted and searched for all of our lives but rarely found.

There was a melodious breeze blowing from someplace deep, and there was fragrance and fields and mountains stretching over vast untold distance. There were bees buzzing and birds singing and beautiful green stars racing across a firmament unseen by the eyes of mortal man. And this is where Carlo said goodbye to Jean.

I sat in the boat and waited. Jean had come to life again. She smiled at Carlo and threw her arms around him one last time and whispered something so sweet in his ear that he simultaneously burst into tears. They held each other for indeterminate moments before she pulled away and ran across the flowered fields, destination unknown. Her spirit free again at last.

Carlo watched her go for a long time, until she was but a faraway speck. He wiped his eyes and came back to me.

"I almost hate to leave, Carlo," I said.

He smiled and extended his hand. "You're not leaving."

A cold shiver of realization shot up my spine and I began to stutter. "I…I don't know, Carlo. Come on…we should go back home."

"Do you really want to go back?"

I thought for a second and I guess that I really didn't. Then Carlo smiled at me and held his hand out again and I understood. I remembered the Bearded Lady's tears falling on my face like drops from the summer ocean and I remembered the blackness that overtook me when I fought with The Fire Eater and it all began to make sense.

So I stayed.

And Carlo returned to the land of the living. I stood on the bank of the river and watched the ferryman pole him back across, into that other land. Once he turned around and waved at me. I waved back, then I headed into the lush paradise that now belonged to me. I walked forever. Then I took a nap beneath a tree draped with white perfumed blossoms…the sweetest you ever smelled.

****

I think about Carlo sometimes, about his great love for Jean and I think about the carnival and the world of misfits I used to live in, and it all seems to hang on for a moment.

But only for a moment, then it's gone.

Because that body isn't me anymore, and it's not Jean, either. My memories fade a little, but never really go away. It's just that I don't need them much anymore. They're like clutter in the attic. I'm a new creature. I walk paths that we all will walk together one day, and I smile in the face of Eternity.

And guess what? Eternity smiles back.

And I hope Carlo, my dear friend, is well…wherever he is…making the big people laugh and leading souls to eternity in the wee strange hours before dawn, and that maybe he's sitting in some lady's tent right now drinking coffee and that maybe, if there is any cosmic mercy out here,

he's in love.

"Santa Claus and Bigfoot Versus Satan"

The snow began to fall again sometime after midnight, blanketing the woods above Three Forks with fresh intricate white flakes that could only have been designed by a higher supernatural brain. The hunter relished in the moment, turning his face up into the misty downpour and smiling to himself like a child drunk on dreams. The thought of the warm sleeping bag that awaited him back at the tent took a backseat to this grandest of wintry spectacles: that of snow falling gently and quietly in the deep woods.

The man pulled his jacket close around his shivering body and sighed. It was beautiful up here in the mountains, away from the city. He had done the right thing by escaping for the weekend. No boss. No phone. No smog or traffic. Los Angeles was far away. A hectic memory to be put on hold for a couple of days. He was here, blissfully alone.

And it was almost Christmas.

He would spend the 24th and 25th in his tent, snowed-in, with some bourbon spiked egg nog and hopefully some fresh venison. Nothing or nobody to answer to but the mountains. The man smiled again as soft flakes of snow danced on his nose.

But the hunter was not alone, as he had thought. There was something else in the woods this night, unbeknownst to him. Something as ancient as the land itself and as mysterious to humans as life after death or outer space.

The wind blew gently through the trees, covering his head and coat with snowflakes. The deep woods were like a nineteenth-century bedtime fairytale tonight. There was magic and beauty there. It warmed his soul, despite the cold chill that crept up his back.

Coffee. He needed to make some coffee. The man turned back towards the tent but stopped dead in his tracks. Something moved. Out there. In the trees. He was sure of it.

He was frozen to the spot. An uneasy chill…not a pleasant one like before… came over him and he began to shiver. His eyes darted nervously back and forth past the trees that grew sky high up there. The towering canopy was thick so there was little undergrowth. It was a place where shadows hid between the branches and behind the thick trunks of the old timber. He had always felt at home here. Now something…an unnatural fear…had come from out of nowhere in a few scant seconds and his mind was now plagued with demons and ghosts.

There was a movement again…out there. Something big and dark moved between two trees and vanished down the ridge. He strained to hear. From somewhere in the darkness came the sound of footfalls in the snow, crunching and moving rapidly in the opposite direction. Then it stopped. Whatever it was.

The man listened intently and glanced around. He saw nothing immediately, but a strange sensation swirled behind his eyes and the ends of his hair danced as he realized that someone or something was watching him. He could feel it. All of a sudden, the temperature felt as if it had dropped. His blood felt icily sluggish and his bones ached.

The sound of snow grinding under feet caused him to wheel around. There, on the ridge beyond his camp was a lone figure in the shadow of a giant pine. The figure peered from behind the tree with luminescent eyes and studied him with silent curiosity. It looked like a man…but it was much too large. The thing looked to be at least eight feet tall with broad shoulders and enormous arms that reached down below its waist. Its head brushed the limbs of the pine as it moved forward slowly.

It never took its glowing eyes off him. The distance between them melted away as the thing leaped across the snowy ridge and came to a stop right before the shivering, mumbling hunter, whose mind had suddenly snapped. The beast was covered in black fur and it studied the strange man with all the interest of a scientist discovering a new species.

Then the beast snapped his neck.

****

"Hurry up, you damned drunk!" The store manager was upset again. "I swear...if I could only find someone else...*anyone* else...to play our Santa, you would be out on the street. Where you belong, I might add!"

It was half past six on Christmas Eve and Steve

Duncan was already a good half hour late for his nightly

Santa gig at the downtown department store. This was the big

night. The stores closed promptly at eight and this was the

last chance for parents to bring their little ones to meet Santa.

It was the most important night of his Santa career and he

was late for it.

Steve waved his arms and tried to fan the alcoholic

fumes away from his red suit, which needed a good washing.

He ran past the line of stone-faced adults and excited children

and quickly took his spot in the big chair beside the oversized

Christmas tree that rose halfway to the towering ceiling.

"Sorry I'm late, folks," he shouted in a hoarse voice. "My

reindeers were double parked."

Nobody laughed. The irate manager, Mr. Goodman,

rolled his eyes and stormed away. Steve knew he was

pushing his luck. He had been late twice this week already.

His intentions were always good. But Happy Hour always called to him and he always answered. It was in his DNA. This inability to turn down a good time.

Steve, the Santa Claus of the hour, adjusted his beard, sat down in his Yule throne that sat in a corner of the store, bedecked in blinking multicolored lights and plastic snow. He adjusted his coat and beard and waved on the first child in line. The little boy turned loose from his mother and raced towards the red suited Steve and bounced into his lap. Steve groaned in pain and tried to shake it off. He faked a smile as the half gallon of cheap rum bubbled up from deep inside his stomach. He belched and pointed at the camera in front of them. The child's excited eyes followed his red gloved finger to the camera lens. The photographer raised a hand and let it fall just as quickly and when the flash went off, Steve's eyes resonated in an agonizing blue haze that wracked his swimming head.

"Oh, god," he moaned, his belly trembling.

The child gazed upwards into Steve's eyes and studied them intently for an instant before he burst into tears and began howling like a wounded animal. Steve placed a finger up to the boy's lips and tried to calm him, but it was no use. The mother rushed over to Santa's chair and glared at Steve. "What did you do to my baby?"

Steve was beside himself. *"I...I..."* He watched helplessly as the irate woman dragged her son away. After surviving another disgusted glance from the store manager, he readied himself for the next child in line and waved a little girl in pigtails and a scarf over. She climbed into his lap, grinned for the photo and proceeded to tell Steve what she wanted for Christmas.

"I want a brand-new doll…the kind that smiles and talks and wets their pants…"

Steve fought back the nausea that was rumbling in his belly. He managed to chuckle. "Santa could probably arrange that."

"…and I want a new cook set…with pots and pans and skillets…so my dolls an' me can have dinner parties…"

"Got it, chickie…now you have a real Merry…"

"…an' I want a giant teddy bear…big enough to fill up my room…"

"Yeah…yeah…Merry Christ…"

"And I want…"

Steve's head was throbbing and all the rum inside him roared like a volcano, waiting to erupt. "That's great, little girl…now Santa has to…"

"…a new daddy."

Steve stopped and looked deep into the little girl's eyes. "You want a *what*?"

"A new daddy. Mine's a drunk and beats my mommy alla time. I want a new daddy who's nice and treats my mommy like a lady."

Steve's eyes became redder and the stinging salt of his tears surprised him as the water rolled down his face. "Santa…will do his best, honey. Santa will do his best for you…okay?"

The girl's face lit up like a brand-new Christmas tree and she threw her arms around Steve's neck. "Oh, thank you, Santa! Thank you!" She jumped from his lap and ran to her mother and the two of them vanished into the crowd. Steve watched them go with his heart following close behind. "Poor kid," he whispered. "Poor kid."

The unsavory glance from his employer snapped Steve back to attention and he motioned for the next child in line. A little boy who wasn't so little raced over to him and jumped into his lap as if he were doing a cannonball in the swimming pool. The impact jostled Steve's insides and started a violent gastro-tremor and this time he could not quell the inevitable spewing of his guts.

The little boy screamed in horror and a shocked hush settled over the crowd as Steve…Santa Claus…opened his mouth and projectile vomited across the store. The boy jumped from Santa's lap and ran for the safety of his mother's arms as she frantically wiped the flecks of bile and half-digested salami from her boy's sweater vest. She glanced up at the manager as he passed and screamed, "You will be hearing from my attorney!"

Steve rose slowly and took one step from the platform where he sat before slipping in his own vomit and falling flat on his back. The crowd that had stood in stunned silence a moment ago now broke out into uproarious laughter at the unexpected spectacle. A dozen onlookers gleefully filmed the scene with their phones as Mr. Goodman stormed over to his prostate Santa with red face and clenched fists and the volcanic fury of Vesuvius building up inside his pounding brain. *"Get out! Get out now! You're fired!"*

Steve picked himself up and stood there wobbling as a tirade of anger and frustration hit him dead in the face. "Sorry, Mr. Goodman…really…I…"

"You have ruined Santa Claus for all of these children and made our store into a laughingstock…you drunken idiot…now get out!"

"Yeah…okay…I'll go," Steve muttered, with tears of anger welling up in his bloodshot eyes. "But you just remember that this is the season of cheer…and of forgiveness…"

"What do *you* know about Christmas, you sot! Get out!" Goodman shouted as he shoved Steve towards the front entrance. His arms flayed about in wild abandon and the veins in his bald head bulged out to the extent that Steve feared the man would drop dead of an aneurysm any second.

"I'll go…but I'll make this the best Christmas ever…you'll see, Goodman! You'll see! I *am* Santa!"

Goodman motioned for security and two uniformed guards rushed over to take Steve by the arms. They escorted him through the front doors and deposited him out on the sidewalk.

"Don't come back," one of them said with a sneer.

Steve stood on the sidewalk with the snow coming down in slow motion flakes. The snow softly blanketed the sidewalk and street in front of the department store and all across the downtown world turning the city into a white wonderland of Christmas dreams and cheer. And Steve felt it more than anyone, despite his vomit caked beard and his wounded pride. Visions of the sad little girl who wanted a new father and a new life came reeling back to him then and he felt himself attuned to all the sufferers lost somewhere out there in the snowy night. "You'll see," he repeated to no one in particular. "I'll make this the best Christmas ever!"

People glanced sideways with curiosity at Santa Claus as he stormed away, trudging through the gathering snow to his car. Steve turned a corner, shielding his eyes from the snow, which was falling harder and harder and obscuring his wobbling vision. A strange figure appeared from out a side alley and bumped into him. Steve drunkenly tipped his red cap. "A thousand pardons, good sir, and a Merry Christmas!"

The figure did not stop or speak. It was a tall man, cloaked in a dark brown robe and cowl with a knotted rope securing the garment around his torso. The man looked like someone out of the Middle Ages. Steve stood there, squinting and trying to see through the misty wall of snow. *"Well, I'll be…"*

Another cloaked figure emerged from the alley and almost knocked Steve down. The robed figure that followed behind did just that. Steve fell face first into the soft snow and lay there with frost caked around his eyes and nose. He watched a line of the robed mystery men walking single file briskly down the street. Something was curiously out of place about them.

Something was awry this snowy night and Steve's alcohol-soaked brain quivered nervously as sober thoughts began to materialize inside the saturated grey matter.

Without another thought, Steve rose from the powdery sidewalk and hurried to catch up to the strange congregation. He raced behind them, following their footprints in the snow. The trail led him down several blocks, around the corner on 33rd and up Beaumont to the warehouse district.

Steve stopped several times to catch his breath. The cold air stung his red face and caused his lungs to ache, but he continued onward. Finally, he saw them turning a corner ahead and he ran up the street, disappearing behind a dumpster to see where they went. The street was a collection of old 1920s warehouses, most of which had been converted into factories and storage space. Many of the old buildings were run down and abandoned. Nobody lived out here, in this decrepit part of town. This was a good place to store illegal goods…or dump a body. A part of town where there were no prying eyes this time of night.

The robed goons vanished into a particularly dark warehouse on the far corner. Steve watched for a long drawn out moment, then he reluctantly moved across the street that was covered in undisturbed snow save for the line of determined footprints.

Steve halted at the splintered front door that hung on rusted hinges from some other age. He adjusted his vomit caked beard and thought long and hard. He leaned in and placed his ear against the door. Inside there was the shuffling of feet and the murmured drone of voices. Steve's brain reeled with curiosity and fear. Who were these people?

This was bizarre. Just plain nutty. But Steve felt a need to investigate the phenomena. It wasn't like he was ditching work or anything. He smiled. That bastard Goodman. He would show him. Steve would perform the greatest and most selfless Christmas act of humanity ever…and Goodman would drown of shame in his own holiday punch. Maybe these robed guys were the ticket. Maybe they were a weird gang of pseudo-Grinches up to no good.

Steve stiffened up and shivered when he heard the woman's scream from inside. He placed his ear closer to the door and waited. Another scream rang out. They had somebody in there…doing horrible things to her! He ran around to the back, banging his knee on an overstuffed garbage can on his way through the side alley. When he reached the back of the old warehouse, he tripped over the curb of the loading dock obscured by the snow. He landed on his face again and thanked his good fortune that the snow had cushioned his fall.

The man in the dirty Santa Claus suit rose and studied the outside of the warehouse. He moved around to the side and found a rust colored windowpane that had lost its glass decades ago. He slowly brushed the broken shards and the debris away from the concrete sill and quietly slipped inside. The snow blanketed the back room and allowed him silent entry into a most forbidding place.

It was pitch black inside and the icy wind blew through the open window and the adjoining rooms like solemn phantoms intent upon one last Christmas haunt before vanishing into the dawn to come. Steve's eyes finally adjusted to the darkness and he moved stealthily into the black pit belly of the abandoned warehouse just as another terror-stricken scream iced his spine.

The woman sounded as if she was being tortured.

And there were intermittent sounds…like a chorus…that started and stopped. It sounded like a monastery, only more sinister. Steve inched his way along the shadowed walls and across the debris littered floors as more screams followed. Soon he saw a light in an adjoining room. It was dim at first but grew brighter as he moved closer. Soon all that separated him from the mysterious band of hooded freaks was a concrete block wall. Dozens of candles burned brightly through an open doorway and he could hear their voices plainly now.

He plastered his body against the wall and peeked through the doorway. A bewildered woman lay on a table. Her hands and feet were tied. Several men in cowls stood ceremoniously around her with their hands folded. The faces were completely hidden.

The woman screamed again as the robed figures began to chant in a monotone drone that sent shivers reeling over Steve's body. It was a positively eerie sound that wasn't from this world. Steve watched on in confusion and fear. What the hell was this?

The candles shivered in the cold wind that blew through the warehouse from outside. The light shimmered, casting weird shadows that writhed and scratched up the walls. It looked like a tomb in there. A mad, forgotten corner of hell.

Steve adjusted his beard and wracked his brain, searching for a plan. He inched his way forward and peered around the edge of the doorway to get a better view of the room and what he saw chilled his blood.

He heard another voice. A smaller voice. A child's voice. It started to come back to him. He recognized the woman on the table suddenly. He had seen her earlier that very evening. At the store. He winced with pain. There was a commotion a few feet from the table. The robed goons were trying to restrain a little girl. The same girl that had looked in Steve's eyes and told him that she wanted a new daddy for Christmas! His heart plummeted down into his stomach and the emptiest feeling he had ever felt blasted him right in the teeth.

"*My God,*" he whispered to the night!

The goons held her fast. She couldn't break free. One of the figures stepped forward and removed something from his robe. Steve gasped when he realized that it was a long-bladed knife! The chanting grew louder and more frantic as the man with the knife drew closer to the table. He stood over the woman and raised his arms in supplication to some unseen deity or force. The knife's blade gleamed in the candlelight. Steve's heartbeat like a jackhammer and thoughts swirled through his skull like a runaway train. He had no clue as to what the hell to do. But he had to do something.

It was obvious what the knife-wielding fiend's intentions were. The robed man raised the knife high above the woman. Her eyes were now glazed over with complete and utter horror. Steve had never witnessed anyone about to die. There was absolutely no doubt in the woman's mind that she was about to feel that sharp blade plunge deep into her breast. She knew. And it was terrible to see.

The little girl struggled in vain to break away from her captors. But she wasn't strong enough. She screamed. *"Leave my momma alone!"*

Steve could wait no longer. He burst screaming into the room and knocked the man with the knife down. He kicked the man in the head with his black boot and quickly grabbed the blade, waving it in the direction of the others as they tried to rush him. The shock of seeing Santa Claus descend out of the shadows to interrupt their ceremony was almost too much, but the unholy goons soon regained their senses. They backed away when they saw that Steve meant business.

Steve cut the woman's bonds and helped her up from the table. The robed acolytes released the little girl and she raced over to her mother. The two embraced and started moving towards the door. "Let's get out of here," Santa Claus said. He waved the knife at the goons again and kept them at bay. The faceless creatures snarled and wailed in protest, but there was little they could do. The man who had wielded the knife rose from the floor and pointed at Steve defiantly. "*You will regret this, infidel! No one interrupts Satan's wedding!*"

"I would offer you congratulations," Steve said as he whisked the woman and girl through the darkened rooms, en route to the night outside and freedom. "But I get the impression that this was an arrangement you didn't quite agree to."

"You would be right," the woman said tearfully. "I don't know what happened…we left the department store and these crazy people grabbed us right off the street…"

Steve stumbled over a 2 x 4 on the dark floor but regained his balance and the three burst out into the snowy night with the Satanists in determined pursuit. The woman gasped as the cold air filled her lungs. She clutched her daughter close to her and pulled her along as they raced down the white blanketed streets, completely devoid of life at this late hour. The three escaped the horrors of the abandoned warehouse and headed for the populated side of town, where safety awaited them.

Steve's mind still boggled at the events of this remote place. It was like a bad dream. For a second, he wondered if all this was nothing more than an alcoholic delirium, but the stinging cold air and the angered voices rising up into the darkness behind them snapped him back to reality. This was happening. Every horror movie square inch of this craziness.

Steve grabbed the woman by the wrist and led her down an alley and around the next corner. She slid in the snow but caught herself and pulled her little girl along behind her. Steve was amazed at the stamina that had come out of nowhere. He felt as if he had run a marathon. He didn't even feel drunk anymore. Almost. Fear could work miracles. "A few more blocks," he reassured her.

The robed goons were back there, howling like a pack of demons. Chasing them through the snowy streets. Howling for their blood.

Beaumont Avenue appeared out of the mist and Steve breathed a sigh of relief. 33rd was next, then the downtown district and the police station. They were almost there. The woman slammed into him and almost fell. She was exhausted. So was the little girl. The child moaned and fell to her knees in the snow. Steve grabbed her up and kept running. "Come on, dear…don't stop now. We're almost there."

The streetlamps outside of the police headquarters shone like a beacon in the swirling mist of falling snow. Steve and the girls left a deep line of footprints as they raced up the front steps. Steve's heart warmed automatically as they stumbled through the front door and saw a surprised officer staring back at them from behind the desk.

The woman collapsed into a chair and Steve placed the girl in her lap. He turned to the officer. "Thank God! We need help, officer…"

The officer eyed them suspiciously and Steve wished suddenly that he wasn't dressed like Santa Claus. "Yes? What's the problem?"

"We just escaped a cult of devil worshippers…they tried to sacrifice this woman here," Steve shouted as he pointed at the woman behind him.

The policeman stared at Steve as if he was measuring him for a straitjacket. "I see…could you hold on a second? I'll be right back." The officer rose and disappeared into the next room.

Steve turned to the woman with a confused look on his face. She returned his glance and he shrugged. The officer returned a second later with a detective in a suit. The detective walked out from behind the desk and stood before Steve with a distrusting glare in his eyes. "Can I help you?"

"You sure can, friend…we just escaped a satanic cult who almost stabbed this woman here to death. If you will get your car, I can show you where they were holed up…"

"That won't be necessary," the detective said matter-of-factly. "You're that department store Santa who was escorted out earlier tonight, aren't you? For being drunk on the job?"

Steve shrank then, almost falling into a chair. The air and the spirit left him completely and he retreated into a shell. The department store Santa lowered his head and nodded, shamefaced and forlorn.

The woman rose and started to protest, but the detective cut her off. "It's Christmas Eve and we're very busy. I think it's pretty obvious what has occurred here. Santa Claus here had a few too many and…"

"No! He's telling the truth!" The woman's eyes grew wide and her face turned blood red.

"Get the hell out of here before I charge you both with public drunkenness," the detective shouted, livid with rage.

Steve took the woman by the arm and led her outside. "Let's go. They're not gonna listen to us." They stopped on the steps and stared at one another in disbelief.

"What do we do now?"

Steve thought for a moment. "Do you have a cell phone?"

The woman nodded. She took the phone from her jeans and handed it to Steve. He searched information and quickly dialed a number. His fingers shook from the cold and the breath rose in great wisps of ghostly steam from his nose and mouth. "The police department in the next county over might be more willing to listen to us."

A tall shadow came out of nowhere and knocked the phone from Steve's trembling hand before the call could be completed. Something caught him on the jaw and knocked him flat. Steve faded into unconsciousness. The last thing he heard was the woman's screams.

****

Steve, Santa Claus, opened his eyes and found himself in a jail cell, lying on a cot against the wall. He groaned. The room moved every time he tried to raise his head. His jaw hurt. Once the room stopped spinning, he began to take inventory of his surroundings. The ceiling…the floor…the walls. None of it seemed real, but yet, it was more real than anything he had ever experienced. The realization hit him suddenly that he had not had a drink for a long indeterminate length of time. He smacked his dry lips and rubbed his aching stomach. For a few seconds, he wondered if he was dead. But the sharp pain and nausea he felt dispelled that theory. He was very much alive and in a bad damn spot to top it all. The detective and three uniformed officers stood over him with a weird fire burning in their eyes. Steve sat up and stared back at them. "What the hell is this?"

The detective grinned. "We're about to take a little ride."

The realization hit Steve like a cannon ball to the face. The policemen unbuttoned their sleeves and raised their forearms to display identical tattoos…a five-pointed star encircled by flames.

"*My god*," Steve whispered.

"The *wrong* god," the detective laughed. "We made a deal with the true entity and His Dark Highness will soon oversee the city, then the county, then the state. After that…the world!"

"And those robed weirdos…"

The detective shook his head. "This conversation is over. You know too much. You have to die."

"The woman and the girl?"

"We will take care of them."

"*You bastard*!" Steve shot out of the bed like a bolt of lightning, but he was knocked out by one of the officers before he could get his hands around the smirking detective.

"Grab him," the detective said. "I'll bring the car around back."

****

Consciousness came reeling back to Steve a little later and it plunged him into a deeper realm of pain he hadn't bargained for. He sat up slowly and moaned. His head ached. His jaw and skull were both swollen and tender. They had hit him hard. Too hard. The pain he felt earlier was just a warm-up. Yes, he was definitely alive. Dead folks didn't hurt like this. Santa rubbed his face and stared out at the night melting past the backseat window. His current situation would be remedied, his status changed, because there was a strong possibility that he wouldn't be alive much longer.

"Well," a voice said. "Look who's awake!"

Another voice said, "Shit. I was hoping he wouldn't wake up. Now he's gonna know what we're gonna do to him. That makes it tougher."

The driver laughed. There were only two cops in the front seat. The dashboard light bathed their faces in shadow and a weird green glow. The combination made them look demonic. Devil worshipping cops. Who would've ever guessed?

Steve adjusted his dirty white beard. He frantically searched his mind for a plan. The woods, dark and snowy, passed by the side windows. They were taking him out in the mountains to do their dirty work. He would vanish from the world of the living and some hunters would find his bones in twenty years or so.

Christmas music was on the radio. "Jingle Bell Rock" melted into "Have Yourself A Merry Little Christmas" and that rolled into "Little Drummer Boy." The cops were silent. They were listening to holiday music and they were taking him out into the middle of nowhere to off him and dump his body. Because he had discovered their little devil-cult. On Christmas Eve of all nights.

It was insane.

Wet flakes of snow began to pelt the window. "It's snowing again," one of the cops observed.

"Good. The snow'll cover Santa Claus up good. They won't find his ass until next spring."

Steve smiled from behind his dirty beard. "You know…you let me go and I'll be sure to leave something in your stockings tonight."

The two cops burst out into laughter. "You're funny, Santa."

"No, seriously. What would you like?"

"A fifth of good premium bourbon," the driver said.

"The keys to a brand-new Porsche," the other cop laughed. "And a pound of top shelf coke."

"Trust Satan," the first cop said with a smile. "He'll give you those things."

Steve cringed. "Can I ask you boys something?"

"I guess so. You are entitled to one last request."

"Why would anybody worship the devil? I mean…there's only one way that's gonna end up…"

"Yeah? How's that, Santa?"

"Roasting marshmallows in a burning pit of fire…"

"Maybe, Santa…but we get everything we want between now and then. Money, girls, cars, houses. More than any runty drugstore Santa that smells like a cheap bar can give us," the cop on the rider's side said with a laugh.

"*Know what, fuckers*?" Steve shouted.

"What, you dumb bastard?"

"You just made Santa's naughty list!" Steve sprang forward and smashed the heads of both officers together with his black gloved hands. Both collapsed into the seat. The car spun out of control and crashed into s snowdrift.

Steve kicked open the back door and ran away into the dark woods.

He heard the dazed cops coming to back at the car. They emerged, shouting frantically and drawing their guns. A bullet whizzed over Steve's head. He screamed in terror and lost his footing. He rolled down into a tree-lined gulley and scrambled in panic through the snow up the other side.

They weren't far behind him. Cold blind fear began to overtake Steve as the corrupt cops hunted him in the woods. He had to put distance between them. And he had to lose that damned red suit that glowed in the snowy woods like a kid's night light.

Steve lost himself in the cold shadows. He backed deeper into the trees until he bumped against what he immediately thought was the thick trunk of a fir or a pine. He pushed against the tree and tried to hide himself in the cover of its low hanging branches. He could see the beams of their flashlights slicing through the mountainous dark and the snowstorm. He could hear their frustrated voices growing closer and louder as they called to one another. Any moment they would be within range of his hiding spot and if the angels didn't favor him, he was a dead man tonight.

Steve pushed closer into the massive tree trunk behind him. He waited, trying not to breathe. Every mist laden breath rose into the air. A direct giveaway. He closed his eyes and tried to stay still. They were close now.

Steve opened his eyes and his heart stopped beating. He searched his thoughts, trying to make sure he wasn't hallucinating. But there was no doubt of it. The tree behind him *moved*.

He reached back to reassure himself that there actually was a tree there. His shaking fingers groped and probed. White-hot fear electrified his addled brain suddenly and he howled in terror as his fingers touched what could only be *fur*…thick fur from a *living* creature! The beast behind him took a step forward and knocked Steve to the ground. He hit the snow and rolled over quickly. Great electric blue waves of lightning shot through him as he looked up…up…into the burning yellow eyes of a thing so massive and primitive that it defied the very intellect that now beheld it. It was true. All true. *"Sasquatch,"* Steve whispered!

The beast stared down at the ramshackle Santa Claus with a quizzical glare stretched across its wide face. A low growl left its throat as it tried to decide whether this intruder was a threat or merely an inconvenience. Or possibly even food.

The sudden sound of voices caused Bigfoot to forget about the prostrate Santa temporarily. It took a few steps forward in the snow and stopped when the two cops came up over the edge of the snow filled gully. They froze in their tracks and stood there with jaws hanging open and arms hanging limply by their sides. One of them screamed and fired his pistol.

The bullets whizzed harmlessly past Bigfoot's head. The primordial guardian of the mountains stood stone still for a confused moment, contemplating the strange invaders of his home until it could no longer contain the mounting anger it felt in its savage breast. The ape-like creature rushed the satanic policemen with all the fury of an out of control bull.

One of the cops fired at the beast point blank, but the bullet bounced harmlessly off Bigfoot's thick, fur covered hide. The man howled in disbelief and horror as the creature took his arm in its massive hands and wrenched the limb loose from its socket. A red spout of blood gushed freely from the stump and spattered on the white snow. Bigfoot swung the severed arm by the wrist like a club and caught the cop in the face, breaking his nose and shattering his teeth. The man's face exploded in crimson Technicolor and he collapsed limply into the snow.

The other policeman fled the scene in terror and vanished down the snowy embankment to the waiting road below. Bigfoot pursued him, taking great superhuman leaps through the trees until it caught up to the cop and summarily smashed the man's head into the trunk of the patrol car. Brains and blood and shards of skull erupted all over the back end of the automobile and the faceless corpse, that had been an evil domineering force a scant few seconds ago, slid lifelessly to the pavement, completely and utterly dead to the winter's night. A threat no more.

The sight of the disembodied arm lying in blood covered snow caused Steve's vision to blur and fade into a deep blue nauseous haze, but he maintained consciousness and glanced up to find Bigfoot looming over him. The giant glared down at the bewildered Santa Claus as if it was contemplating what to do with him. Somehow the beast knew that Steve was one of the good ones and no more a threat to it than a moth would be to a lion.

"You really exist!" Steve said under his breath. It was amazing. A legend come to life right before his eyes…and his savior, nonetheless. All those campfire stories were true. The two stared at each other in disbelief. The beast studied him with intelligent eyes. This was no mere monster…the kind that romped across drive-in screens on Saturday nights. This was a thinking being. "You can understand what I'm saying…can't you?"

Bigfoot turned its head side to side. A low growl rolled off its tongue. The creature watched Steve curiously for a moment, then turned and vanished into the trees as easily as it had appeared.

Steve watched Sasquatch go. Then he rose from the snow and shook the dizziness from his head. A newer, more solid resolve came over him when he remembered the woman and her daughter. They were somewhere out there, captive or worse. He had to save them. He was the only one who could. It was Christmas Eve and miracles were still possible.

The keys were still in the ignition. The patrol car started; the engine roared to life. Steve pointed the car towards town and the warehouse district. But would those goons take the woman and the girl back to the same place? Steve groaned. Where could they be?

He pushed on the gas and the car lurched forward into cold space. Even though the mountains were capped with several feet of snow, the roads were clear. Steve was halfway down the mountain when he noticed the unmistakable red glow of taillights disappearing down an unpaved road that snaked through a tall stand of pines. He pulled off on the side

of the road and watched a line of cars moving at a distance

behind the far trees.

There were at least five cars, maybe even a couple of

trucks. Steve put the patrol car in park and turned the ignition

off. He slipped around the back and up a small embankment

into the pines. The moon finally emerged from behind the

clouds and a plethora of stars appeared almost

simultaneously as the winter front moved on down the

mountain. The moonlight gave the snowdrifts beneath the

pines a soft phantom glow.

Steve raced through the stand of trees until he came

out at the old logging road. He followed the fresh vehicle

tracks for a quarter mile until he came to a large wooden

structure that looked as if it had been used to house road

equipment, probably for the highway department. He looked

cautiously around him then bolted across the white expanse

of a cleared field to the shed. He pinned himself to the side wall and placed his ear to the wood.

Several muffled voices filled his ears. There was a commotion, lots of milling around. Steve glanced at the row of vehicles parked in front. Several police cars. Two or three big trucks. His heart sank when the front door opened, and two robed figures stepped out into the darkness. One of them turned and said, "We will be right back. Don't start without us."

Steve backed farther into the shadows and waited. The voices started again, getting louder and louder. The front door was slightly ajar, and it allowed him to hear more clearly. Several people were arguing. In the midst of the clamor was a woman's voice. It was her…the mother he had rescued earlier. *"Don't! Please…let my daughter go! I won't tell a soul…I…"*

Steve immediately recognized the next voice. "You will not have the opportunity to talk. You know too much, babe. Carter…you wanna do the honors? It's your wife after all."

It was the police detective from the station in town.

"What about the little girl?" Someone else asked.

"What do you think? We sacrifice her…the blood communion," the detective said.

"Why not the woman, too? We were going to before…"

"She's become a nuisance. I'd rather just shoot her and be done with it. The girl is a better sacrifice anyway. She's innocent. Satan will dig that."

Steve felt a raw surge of anger rifling through him. Those bastards. This shit had gone far enough. Too far, in fact. A strange voice from behind caught him off guard suddenly and made his blood run cold with panic.

"Why don't you go on in?"

Without thinking, Steve threw a roundhouse punch and caught one of the devil worshippers squarely in the face. He felt the man's cartilage shift and the bone in his nose break. The devotee's cowl flew back, and he went down amid a shower of blood. Steve nudged the cowl with the toe of his boot. It was one of the cops from the station. The one at the front desk. He lay sprawled unconscious on his back in the snow. Steve had knocked him out. A proud grin broke across his face. He moved around the side of the storage building and peered through a window near the front. The room was lit by battery operated lanterns placed haphazardly around the room on top of a nearby salt truck, a tractor, and some boxes. There were several hooded cultists standing around the woman, who was tied to a wooden chair. She glanced nervously back and forth at the robed men, whose faces were obsidian shadow masks that gave no clue to their identities. The only one who was not garbed in ceremonial gear was the detective. He sat in a chair across from his prisoner and stared into her eyes like a cat that had cornered the mouse for the final time.

"Carter? Front and center," the detective ordered.

A robed figure moved from the back and came to stand beside the detective, who reached inside his coat and produced a sharp dagger in a leather sheath. He casually removed the sheath and tossed it over his shoulder. The corrupt detective tested the dagger tip on his finger and winced as a blot of red appeared and began to trickle down his hand. "*Ouch*," he laughed.

He handed the razor-sharp dagger to Carter. "Kill her!"

The officer named Carter removed his hood and stood there with his eyes burning fiercely in the light. He took the knife and loomed over the helpless woman. Steve noticed that his hand was trembling. "You just had to poke your nose into our business," Carter said with a stiff upper lip. "If you had just left well enough alone, we wouldn't be here right now."

The woman spat at him. "I don't know which I hate worse…the fact that you are a corrupt cop or the fact that you're a devil worshipping piece of…"

"*Enough!*" The impatient detective reached for the knife. "Give me the damned blade, Carter. I'll do it myself!"

A swirl of regret tore through the officer and that boiled into an outright frenzy of determined anger. Without another thought, he plunged the dagger into the detective's chest. The surprised detective stared wide eyed in shocked silence down at the growing red spot on his white shirt. Then he buckled over and lay still on the floor of the shed.

Steve recoiled in horror as the other cult members threw back their cowls to reveal the true extent of their demonic involvement. With a chorus of dry hisses, they lunged at Carter, who had just betrayed them. Steve had to bite his hand to keep from screaming: Their yellow, cat-like eyes glowed in the semi-light and long fangs protruded from their lips as they pounded upon the hapless policeman, who had redeemed himself at the final moment and died under the white flag of forgiveness.

"I'm sorry, babe!" he screamed at his wife.

The woman threw back her head and sobbed uncontrollably. She wrestled and strained against her bonds, but it was no use. The cultists stood up from their kill, with blood smeared across their devil's faces. Their eyes beamed with evil and their voices sounded like snakes trying to whisper. One of the robed goons pointed at her. *"The woman...let's take her, too, brothers..."*

"No," another replied. "She belongs to Satan. Let us shed her blood in sweet ceremony...as we were bidden to do!"

"Here we go again," Steve moaned. He readied himself for one last gallant rush into the shed screaming like a banshee but the sudden presence of a hand on his shoulder caused him to freeze. And it wasn't just a hand...but an *enormous hand* with long fingers that reached down to his chest.

Steve wheeled around to find Bigfoot looming over him! The beast stared down at him with a benevolent glare across its face. Steve overcame his fears of the unknown and cracked a smile. "You wanna help me?"

Bigfoot growled and its yellow eyes widened.

"Okay then," Steve said slowly. "Those men in there…are evil. They're gonna kill that poor woman and her little girl. We gotta save them. Do you understand?"

Bigfoot growled again. It lurched forward and before Steve could say anything more, the lumbering eight-foot tall creature from the dawn of time burst through the front door and commenced to breaking the place apart. One of the cult members crashed screaming through the side window and landed, a bloody pulp, in the snow.

The scene inside was pure chaos as Steve slipped in, untied the woman, and led her away. Bigfoot smashed one of the devil-men into the side of a snowplow and broke his neck. The great beast of the woods threw another man down and stomped a hole in his guts, then grabbed the next man and hurled him like a feather pillow against the wall. The entire building shook with the impact and the man moved no more. Another man leapt upon the Sasquatch's furry back and tried to use a stranglehold. But the effort was useless, and Sasquatch threw the man on the ground and crushed his skull flat with its giant legendary foot. Brains and blood splattered out the top of the man's head and coated the nearby tractor's tire.

Steve took the woman to safety and ran back inside to find Bigfoot turning around in confusion. The beast surveyed all the damage and stood there wanting more.

"Just getting started, eh, boy-o? Well, it's okay…we won. All the bad guys are dead. You did a fantastic job." Bigfoot looked at his unlikely ally, the man in the Santa Claus outfit, and growled in agreement.

There was a sudden stirring amidst the pile of dead bodies and pure unadulterated horror came rushing up at

Steve as he recognized the dead detective, rising up from death, a demon possessed shell. Steve screamed as the living corpse threw an open hand in Bigfoot's direction and by the power of some weird unseen force, sent the giant reeling against the wall! The detective rose and came right at Steve. He grappled the department store Santa by the throat and lifted him, kicking and gagging into the air.

The corpse's voice boomed across the storage shed as if it were being fed through speakers. "Did you *really* think you could beat us? Did you *really* think that a cheap drunk and a furry sideshow freak could beat the awesome power of Satan and his disciples?"

The detective gestured to the corner of the shed and there sat several wooden crates. "You see that? Its bombs, you dumb bastard! Satan is going to blow up City Hall and take over the city! Tomorrow it's another city, then Los Angeles, then the world! Satan is going to create a world dominated hierarchy of evil and we are going to rule for two thousand years!"

Steve tried to retort, but the detective's vise-like fingers squeezed the air and vocals right out of him. So he brought his boot up and caught the detective in the guts. And that wasn't appreciated. The living corpse raised its eyebrows and a strange light came from its pupils. In no time at all, the detective rose steadily into the air, carrying Steve higher and higher, until they almost reached the dark wooden rafters of the ceiling.

The detective's flesh became a sickly black/green and his eyes became endless pits of flame. Horns sprouted from his forehead and talons stretched from his hands, digging into Steve's neck. Steve was forced to experience this terrible transformation! He screamed as the detective's voice grew deeper and more distorted. *"Don't ever kick me again, mortal,"* the monster screamed! Great and horrible blasts of hot air rushed from its mouth and singed the fake beard hanging limply from Steve's face.

The devil-beast jerked forward suddenly, and Steve glanced down to see Bigfoot wrapping its massive arms around the horrible entity, shaking it violently as if it wanted to dislodge a coconut from the top of a towering palm tree.

The demon rushed down to the ground with lightning speed. Steve collapsed to the floor with his head reeling and his stomach rising up into his mouth. He rolled over on the ground and tried to regain his senses. Above him the Battle Royale was erupting.

Bigfoot tackled the supernatural thing and dug its thick fingers into the detective's eyes. Even though the ocular cavities were now balls of fire, the attack still caused the demon pain and it lashed out with everything it had. Bigfoot was knocked flat but sprang back immediately with even more rage. The hairy beast pummeled the green demon with its big fists and the satanic entity felt every blow. It wailed in pain and struggled to fend off the brutish anthropoid. Bigfoot sailed through the air again, head over feet, and landed with a crash on the other side of the shed. But the beast sprang up once again and rushed the demon. Bigfoot tackled the thing just as it began to rise to the ceiling again.

"How does it do that?" Steve cried out in amazement.

The demon carried its hairy foe to the ceiling like a rag doll and simultaneously released its hold on Bigfoot. Steve gasped as his newfound ally plunged to the ground twenty feet below with arms and legs flaying around. Steve heard the woman scream from behind him. He turned to find her staring in horror at the demonic detective and the giant man-thing plummeting to earth.

Bigfoot hit with a great crash. A massive cloud of dust rose from the spot and the giant did not move. The demon's hands rushed through space like a rubber band and grabbed Steve up into the air. It lifted the stunned Santa up to the ceiling and held him there. Steve closed his eyes and prepared himself for certain death. The demon laughed menacingly, and Steve felt its burning brimstone breath drawing nearer and nearer.

What happened next is branded into Steve's memory forever. The overpowering sound of jingle bells came out of nowhere and caused Steve to open his eyes. Then came a resounding thud as something massive landed on the roof. He looked at the demon who had paused to glance upwards in confusion at the ceiling. Something unexpected was happening and the demon didn't know what to make of it.

A moment later the front door burst open again and a fat man in a red suit strolled casually through the door with a large sack thrown across his shoulder. Behind him came a line of small statured guys dressed in green suits with small bells jangling from their hats. They could only be elves!

Steve's eyes grew large and when he opened his mouth a hoarse croak came out. *"Santa…?"*

The one true Santa Claus placed the sack carefully on the ground and looked up at the towering demon. "I will thank you to release my employee this moment, sir!"

An evil grin broke across the demon's face. "No problem."

Before Steve knew what was happening, he was tumbling through the air, en route to a jarring finish on the hard ground. But out of nowhere came the sound of a tightly coiled spring being released and Steve was caught mid-air by something large and padded. He was placed gently on the ground and looked over to see a grinning elf operating some kind of giant hand. The amazing contraption had come out of a tiny box carted by Santa's whimsical entourage. Steve sat there in amazement. The woman rushed to his side and both of them watched the proceedings.

Santa's deep voice boomed. "Demon! You aren't going to beat us this night! Go back to Hell where you came from and leave these fine folks alone! Santa Claus has spoken!"

One of the elves reached into his pack and removed a red ball, which he hurled ninety miles an hour at the demon's head. There was an explosion and a thick green mist filled the demon's face with an unknown substance that automatically sent the fiend into convulsions of coughing and gagging. Green vomit splattered like rain drops over the heads of Steve and the woman. The humans screamed and tried to shield themselves. A mystical umbrella appeared out of nowhere and protected the humans from the devil's rain.

Steve opened his eyes to see a grinning elf close by wielding the magical red Yuletide parasol.

The demon gained its composure, however, and smiled as it opened its jaws wider and sprayed hundreds of gallons of spewing foamy bile at Santa Claus and his brave helpers. Onc of the elves quickly opened his bag and waved a sparkling neon green shield of light in the direction of the demon. The glow quickly covered Santa and his elves. The vomit bounced harmlessly from the protective shield and landed in sizzling pools on the ground.

"*Very clever, Santa,*" the demonic behemoth howled in a soul shattering voice that shook the earth all the way up to the rafters. "But you won't beat us! Remember that *Santa* also spells *Satan*!" The demon rolled its clawed hands together as if rolling cookie dough and a red flaming ball appeared between its fingers. The thing hurled the ball towards Santa and his elves and just before the missile hit, the flames split into letters that spelled the name of the most unholy angel in history: *Satan*.

There was an explosion. Santa Claus and the elves flew sprawling from the impact and landed on their backs. The demon was beside itself with mirth. *"Take that, you fat bastard*!" It laughed.

The breath caught in Steve's throat as the demon then turned its attention towards them. He pulled the woman close to him and held her tight as the towering thing before them rolled another fireball between its claws. Steve glanced back at the door…there was no possible way they would make it before the beast's firepower shredded them. Regardless of that grim fact, they had to try. He rose quickly and pulled the woman along. He could feel the ground quaking in anticipation of the demon's wrath. They were going to die…but at least they would die on their feet, in the act of escaping.

Steve and the woman raced for the open doorway. When he glanced back, Steve saw the demon's arm raised and a swirling mass of flame and wind aimed in their direction. Santa and his elves were out of commission. They were red and green blobs of smoking meat, lying defeated and heart wrenchingly still at the demon's feet.

Steve and the woman made one final leap for freedom just as the air began to stir and the temperature began to rise inside the shed. They landed on their feet outside and raced for the trees beyond and stopped to catch their breaths. Steve hugged his knees and wretched his fevered guts out, then he stood up and looked back at the shed in confusion. An orange glow emanated around the roof and through the doorway and windows. All of a sudden there was a great concussion and an inhuman roar that tore apart the night with a violent and savage tempest of sound and force.

The demon's firebomb never came.

But there was a struggle going on in there. "Wait here," Steve told the woman. He raced back towards the shed and stopped in front of the doorway. Inside there was a battle raging the likes of which mankind had never witnessed. Bigfoot was *not* dead. The creature had regained consciousness and was attacking the demon with unbridled ferocity. Steve gasped at the force of the blows Sasquatch landed on the demon's flesh. Again and again the beast pummeled Satan's handyman with its massive right fist. The demon howled with surprise and pain and tried to muster enough concentration to blast Bigfoot into another dimension, but the mountain creature would give the demon no quarter nor enough time to forge any semblance of concentration so it could work its dark magic. Bigfoot swung the demon viciously in a circle by its right arm, causing the devil-beast to lose its self-control and its form. The demon convulsed and wailed in terror as its body expanded and contracted in a cartoonish, out-of-control whirlwind spectacle until it went sailing across the shed and crashing into the far wall.

Steve ran over next to Bigfoot and the two allies waited for the demon's next move. But they were surprised to find only a shattered corpse that rose from and confronted them with quivering blank eyes. No longer a twenty-foot tall demon. No longer a threat. Or so they momentarily thought.

When Bigfoot took another step towards the detective, the living dead man raised his hands in defiance. Something…an unseen force that was incomprehensible to Steve…throttled both Steve and his simian compatriot. The two of them clutched at their throats and struggled to breathe as the possessed detective squeezed tighter and tighter. Steve fell to his knees and tried to deflect the monster's grip, but there was nothing tangible to fight. This was something wholly supernatural and it could not be beaten on Steve's limited terms.

Steve's vision was turning blue. He could not last much longer. His lungs burned with fire and his brain pulsed with a white-hot panic. The shed…the corpse standing across the room…all was beginning to fade away. Death was near.

There was a commotion suddenly and a multitude of voices. At first Steve thought that he was listening to a chorus of angels shouting, but the deafening report of gunfire snapped him back to reality and he dropped to the ground as the detective's psychic grasp was broken.

It was Santa Claus and his elves. They had regained consciousness and had somehow rigged a large machine gun of some sort and were blasting the detective into minestrone soup! The sack that Santa had carried in with him lay deflated on the ground. Steve laughed. The jolly old bastard had carted in a veritable Christmas arsenal with him! And he knelt on the ground as the elves helped him support the damned thing and fed a cartridge belt into the gun's side. His long white beard danced about on his chest as he fired.

The detective's body jerked forward and backward and side to side as the bullets cut into it and filleted its dead flesh, severed limbs, and perforated organs with deadly accuracy. And then it was over. The smoke cleared and all that remained of the detective was a pile of smoldering meat.

Santa tilted the gun's red-hot barrel towards his face and blew the smoke away in a fitting and ceremonial end to the fracas. "Nobody screws with the man in the sleigh!" he said with the jolliest laugh Steve had ever heard. The elves began to cheer and hop around in merriment.

Santa turned to the bewildered Steve and said, "Merry Christmas to you Steve…keep fighting the good fight!"

Steve was nearly speechless. "It's *you*…it's really you. And you just killed the devil!"

"Oh, that wasn't the devil, Steve…just one of his helpers. Satan can't come out on this holiest of nights. He sends his peons to do his dirty work." Santa glanced over at the wooden crates, stuffed with bomb makings. "Well, well. Those bastards were really going to take over the city, weren't they?" He snapped his fingers and the bombs vanished into thin air. "That should take care of that."

Santa tipped his cap to the woman and Bigfoot. "Merry Christmas to you all…and to all of you…a good night!" He turned to go and paused. "You know, Steve…you really are the true spirit of Christmas. You listen to all the city's children…to their problems…to their wants for Christmas Eve. And not only that…I've never seen anyone so selfless and quick to risk their own personal safety for the benefit of others. You are the heart and soul of the holidays. Don't ever forget it."

Santa smiled and gestured towards the back of the building. "I think someone is ready to be rescued." Steve ran over and found the little girl tied up and lying face down inside one of the snowplows. He opened the door and pulled the child out and untied her. The girl stared at Santa with all the wonder and merriment of childhood in her young face.

The old man reached into his coat pocket and produced a small wrapped package with a shiny red bow. "This is for you, honey. Don't open it till tomorrow." The girl ran over and hugged the old man. "Merry Christmas, Santa and thanks for saving us!" Santa let out a jolly cackle that made his belly shake. He nodded at Steve and Bigfoot. "Well thank you, sweetie…but these guys had a lot to do with it, too!"

Santa Claus looked at his elves. "Shall we go, boys?"

The elves responded unanimously with cheers and laughter. Santa brought his finger up to his nose but paused. "I left something for you in your stocking, Steve."

"Thanks, Santa," the star-struck Steve said sheepishly.

Santa started to touch his nose again but paused for a second time. "Oh…and Steve? Remember…it's a good man that puts others before himself. Don't ever forget that."

"I won't, Santa."

"I'll expect more great things from you next year."

Steve smiled as Santa touched his nose finally and vanished into a twinkling comet's tail of stardust, confetti, and gleaming light that drifted quickly out the shattered window and up the side of the shed.

The bewildered Bigfoot growled and shook its head. The living legend walked out the front door and vanished into the trees. Steve watched the creature go with a slight sadness in his heart. "I wish Bigfoot nothing but peace."

The woman smiled and put her arms around Steve's waist. "Thank you," she said softly.

He pulled the dirty fake beard from his chin and planted a kiss firmly on the woman's waiting lips while the little girl giggled. "Merry Christmas," she said. "Merry Christmas to everybody…to Santa and his elves…and Bigfoot, too!"

Outside a single star from the firmament twinkled. Everything was right with the world.

The End

Neal Privett lives on a farm somewhere in Tennessee, where he writes furiously, drinks too much coffee, and brews horror pulp in the barn. A fan of monsters and rock and roll from an early age, he is co-host of the music podcast, *The Jukebox From Mars*, as well as the horror hosting show on local WEPG television, *Tennessee Macabre*. His stories can be found in anthologies from Pro Se, Sirens Call, and Horrified Press, as well as in the magazines Blood Moon Rising, Schlock!, Lovecraftiana, Weirdbook, and The Horror Zine. More of his novels and short story collections will be forthcoming from Yellow Door Press.